The House
Charlott
Burned

Table of Contents

I dedicate this book to the badly behaved women I have known, and will get to know in my life time.

Every unfeminine act of rebellion fills my heart with a pride that'll see me comfortably through, to my dying days.

For the Charlotte's and the Duffy's out there.

And for Linda.

I love your attitude.

Trigger Warning

The House that Charlotte Burned is a dark story containing themes related to ***sexual abuse, mental health, child abuse, alcohol consumption, death, violence, loss, depression, and sex***.

Reader discretion is advised.

If you find any of these topics distressing or triggering, please consider your well-being before proceeding with this material.

Seek support from a mental health professional or a trusted individual if needed. Your mental and emotional health are important.

Disclaimer

Acknowledgements

I would like to extend my heartfelt gratitude to everyone who contributed to the creation of this book, *The House That Charlotte Burned*. Writing this novel has been an intense labour of love, and I am deeply thankful for the support and assistance that made it possible.

First and foremost, I'd like to express my sincere appreciation to Emruli by Linda Designs for their exceptional talent in designing the captivating book cover. The striking imagery they crafted perfectly captures the seductive essence of this story.

A special thanks to our cover model, Linda Engelbrecht, whose captivating presence breathed life into the characters within these pages. Your grace and poise shine through every portrayal.

I also wish to acknowledge the talented photographer, Chirag Nayak, whose evocative image of fire, sourced from unsplash.com, graces the cover. Your work added a unique and powerful dimension to the book's visual narrative. As well as the immensely gifted photographer, Jonathan Cooper for the contribution of the image he so aptly titled, *Empty Road to Observatory*.

To my beta readers and critique partners, your invaluable feedback and unwavering support have been instrumental in shaping this story. Your dedication to helping me refine and strengthen the narrative is deeply appreciated.

To my family and friends, thank you for your unending patience through countless read throughs, requests for critique and annoying rewrites. Your ceaseless encouragement, support and understanding during the many hours spent at the keyboard and your belief in me and this project has kept me going, even when the writing journey became mind-numbingly challenging.

Lastly, to the readers who adventure with me into this dark tale, your curiosity and passion for stories like these are the heartbeat of the writer's craft.

Thank you for inviting these characters into your hearts. This book is a testament to the collaborative spirit of the creative community, and I am deeply humbled by the generosity and talent that has surrounded its creation.

With heartfelt thanks,

Dihn Bailey

Prelude

Paroxysms, confinements to asylums, rest cures, so many tinctures and snake oils that she no longer sweat clear but a fine orange mist that stained her clothes and bed linens — medical treatments, pelvic massages, and not one bit of it worked.

In the twilight of 1865, amidst the elegant streets of Victorian England, lived a young woman one would deem ahead of her time, named Charlotte. A creature of defiance, she was a silent and relentless rebel against the constraints of her era. Like so many other pretty little English girls, Charlotte had been groomed for a life of submission. Nothing but motherhood and wifery, charities, parties, and pastries would tether her poor soul to the expectations of a society that sought to confine her within the delicate containment of a fragile sensibility.

A hellish existence for women like Charlotte, in short.

But Charlotte harboured secrets from a young age, secrets that flowed as a clandestine river beneath her primed and innocent exterior.

They termed it hysteria, and while they had yet to touch upon the most radical solution for such an illness — a hysterectomy, Charlotte was fast burning through the list of treatments with her unfeminine stubbornness and wayward ways. She raged at her mother, even as a small girl, rebelling against her as Mrs Nicholson dragged her from the candle-lit study in the middle of the night.

"I don't know why you insist on doing this, Charlotte!" She clasped the girl's arm so tightly that it left blue marks for days afterward, "I spend my days teaching you and your sister!"

Catherine Nicholson dragged her ungrateful daughter through the home kicking and screaming until she could not anymore, and, losing her patience, she released her frustrations on the defiant little bitch. Blow after blow landed on Charlotte's determined face and she let them fall, staring furiously at Catherine and not wincing even once.

And when Catherine's arms got tired, Charlotte continued staring her directly in the eye. In the silence that followed the beating on that chilly December evening back in 1865, it became crystal clear that Catherine held no care or love for who Charlotte knew herself to naturally be. The understanding etched itself with the finality of a sharp knife, and both minds were simultaneously made up.

The last resort was not some secret they hid away from Charlotte for her protection — but a threat often used to force her to comply.

In the days that followed that horrendous row, Charlotte had to admit even herself, impressed. She seemed to have won the right to read in peace. As her bruises yellowed and eventually faded, she stayed barricaded and unbothered in her late grandfather's study consuming book after book.

It started as a random throwaway thought, the idea of running away.

She had been lying, sprawled across the threadbare rug in her usual spot with several books thrown out in front of her. Books with ink drawings of medical procedures. Stained books detailing horrific gruesome expressions of pain on the patient's faces and the threat suddenly became a real, tactile danger.

Suddenly, Charlotte's legs began to burn with a hunger to be used. Determined, she shut every single one of those books with a loud and angry thud and placed each carefully back in its place before she began to move methodically through the vast collection pulling out anything and everything she could find about a life of buccaneering.

Days turned into a week, then two, as Charlotte's mind ate the information from every page until she heard it — the familiar and frankly comical clicking of Dr. Grants to big shoes.

He had come to the Nicholson Manor recurrently over the past few months, always on his own, but not this time. This time he brought what sounded like two heavy-set men. This was enough for Charlotte's feet to kick into motion. She fled the grand estate with nothing but the clothes on her back and the black leather-bound book in her hands, tucking it down the front of her nightgown as she clambered out onto the third-floor wrought iron balcony to the icy night and shimmied down the drainpipe, occasionally gripping on the thick vines of ivy that anchored the drainpipe to the brick wall.

Free as a bird, Charlotte ran barefoot through London, all the way to the docks. Temporarily, she traded her life of means and comforts for an uncertain future — but one where she, Charlotte, would decide.

With the knowledge she had so secretly amassed, she embarked on a journey that would take her far beyond the prim and proper world she knew.

Meanwhile, in a different corner of England, another young soul yearned to escape the looming shadow of familial expectation and tradition. William Bennet, the son of a prominent solicitor, Mr Nigel Bennet, felt a discordant note in the symphony of legal texts and courtrooms. His heart thirsted for more, and he was plagued by a passion for minerals and rocks, which began with what is now known as alpinism. The hobby boomed and captivated him instantly after hearing some Swiss boys speak of near-death experiences in their most recent push for a peak so high that the air shredded their lungs. Young and impressionable, William listened as the boys sat drunk and guffawing in a jail cell while he waited for his father.

Soon, he found he could not focus in a classroom. He yearned to feel the wind on his skin and the sun on his face. Golden light plagued his visions in the deepest parts of his slumber. He often awoke sweating and terrified, reaching for something far off. On these lonely nights, William would be left with an empty feeling for hours afterward until sleep reclaimed him. Occasionally, he'd lie there all night, staring beyond the ceiling of his bedroom, sinking deeper into that empty feeling, curious to see where the bottom of the pit lay. It was always coupled with the sweet scent of a flower he could not place — for William had never before smelled anything as stunning.

Instead of pursuing the legal career ordained by his father, and his father before him, William fled after a sudden realisation. It was a singularly warm and clear evening; his parents were throwing one of their usual parties. William had crept up to the roof of their building, desperate for fresh air as the Hudson twins appeared to have marked him the most eligible bachelor in London. Up here, the deep sadness he felt permanently seemed to ebb away, revealing nothing short of disdain for the appearances he was expected to keep up with such a public lifestyle.

Like Charlotte, William felt his feet carry him away from his home that night, but William did not sail away. Instead of suffocating in the warm embrace of his family's stifling expectations, William swore an oath in bitter resentment to celibacy. And with ease, he settled into the refuge within the sacred walls of the Catholic Church, which then put him on to study Geology.

Fate, it seemed, had plans that would unite these two disobedient spirits, for their paths converged in the most unlikely of places: Palestine.

Charlotte, now free and untamed as the wind with an insatiable thirst for adventure, had found her way into the enigmatic world of academia. She found herself attached to an institution dedicated to unravelling the secrets of the Holy Land through her interests. Many of which had spread themselves across the realms of relics and cultural understanding. William, now a wandering soul within the Catholic Church spending his days off in the mountains, had become quite entangled in the Fund's endeavours, owing to his geological pursuits when he noticed her. The most beautiful woman he had ever seen. Charlotte laughed like a man and held herself upright. She wore trousers like men and spoke, unlike any woman he had ever met. In the shadow of history, and the promise of discovery, Charlotte and William's hearts and passions collided, igniting a love that burned with the intensity of a thousand stars. And speaking of stars, the lovers took to gazing at every chance they could, discovering a love of astronomy together. Their connection was instant, and they aligned magnetically.

Together, William and Charlotte embarked on a whirlwind romance, defying the expectations of their respective backgrounds and families. William left the Catholic Church. The two shared a passion for exploration, discovery and the mysteries of the Earth. A bond that far transcended the boundaries of society and faith.

Their love story would carry them far beyond the ancient hills of Palestine, to a land unknown to them both — the Eastern Coast of the Southern tip of Africa. Here, amidst the rolling hills of the midlands and beneath the vast African skies, they would build an observatory where they could live, love, and study the heavens together. It was a place of love and passion where William could finally see the golden light on the air that had plagued him in his sleep. And when the springtime brought the floral blooms, William could finally place that floral scent for the jasmine that lingered in her hair even months after the rains subsided. Their love for each other grew unbreakable as they forged new friendships before they welcomed a daughter - Leila, who had Charlotte's beautiful hazel eyes and stubborn mind.

But fate is a capricious bitch.

Tragedy finally took a running leap at this family and struck down the ship that Charlotte was on when returning from a short trip back to England. She had spent months away from her family convening with certain figureheads at Oxford University. Charlotte's ship met its doom off the treacherous coast of the Cape of Good Hope, sinking to the unforgiving depths of the Atlantic.

Of the few survivors who clung to life's fragile thread, Charlotte was not among them. William scanned every turned-down face on that dock and waited for three more weeks. Eventually, however, he was forced to return home to care for Leila. Beacon extinguished beneath the waves, Charlotte left William with a love that would endure all the suffering it pressed upon the very essence of his being.

Chapter One

He lay on the comfortable carpeted floor of the second landing in the house that he built for Charlotte. Utterly shattered, William stared up at the yellowwood that adorned the ceiling and served as the flooring to the observatory and study where Charlotte spent most of her time.

William had taken special care of the finer details of this house. The young lovers had spent more time dreaming and plotting where to best build their observatory than they had on their wedding — which consisted of a round of drinks at the Bird and Baby. For months in their tiny little London apartment, Charlotte poured over maps, books and pamphlets. All of which cluttered the place so badly that there was barely a place to step.

William recalled the birth of their shared dream, as though it were last night, and he still had the taste of her on his lips. Her silhouette was hugged so tantalisingly by the cotton sheets beneath which she lay naked in the glimmering golden light of the candles that burned day and night in her laboratory.

"I don't think I should chase artefacts much longer." She sighed tiredly at him, cat-like beneath the covers and smoking a cigarette.

"Oh, no?" William chuckled warmly at her. Charlotte would let utter nonsense fall from her lips after their lovemaking, and he highly suspected that she did not wish him to leave. So, he kissed her lips and decided to stay.

"No..." She said, musing offhandedly just millimetres from his lips, her eyes filled with a tenderness so deep that his breathing hitched. Raising her cigarette-free hand to stroke his cheek lovingly, she whispered, "I am certain the ocean will kill me."

In his memory, her eyes filled and glowed with the chuckle that escaped her throat in echoes. Rippling vibrations in his reverie pushed his mind back to absorbing the reality ahead of him.

Every detail of that house was a gift from William to Charlotte. But the wood that adorned so much of the house... That had been for William. He had walked for days and nights, felled many trees as Charlotte documented the landscape and species around them until he found it — the Yellowwood Tree, with its golden wood to carry the light that had so plagued his sleep from his youth into her tents, and now, into their home. And he was living in a dream.

William gasped a horrible sob and shut his eyes, not wanting to look up at the ceiling anymore but finding himself unable to stop. He ached to see the boards disturbed again by her pacing footsteps as she poured over maps and books, plotting their next adventures.

His longing grew more each day until William found he could no longer lie on that floor — he needed to go back to the coast to see her. And, for the seventh time that day, William heaved a sigh, rolled over and raised himself from the floor. Missing Charlotte, he marched determinedly down the stairs of the middle landing and straight towards the front door. That damn golden light streamed through the glass panes. Squinting before reaching up, William plunged his hand down on the handle.

The door was half open when her voice cracked the air like a whip, "WILLIAM!" and he froze in his tracks like a child caught sneaking, "Shut that door! You're not going and spending your days at the coast again!"

Duffy shot him a stern look and stood short and stout in the doorway to the kitchen, hands on her hips and a no-nonsense look etched across her beautifully round and melanin-rich face. Duffy had very symmetrical features and a strong brow line that gave her quite an intimidating aura. There was no forced smile on her face, and he noted the heavy wooden rolling pin in her right hand and shut the door begrudgingly with a gulp.

But she smiled at him comfortingly and held out a hand beckoning him gently to the kitchen, "Come have some tea," he just stood there wordlessly, "come now," she crooned softly, placing her rolling pin down on the counter out of sight to him and hastily wiped her hands before stepping up to him and putting her arm around his shoulder, gently pushing him away from the door and to the kitchen.

Their kitchen, though cluttered and overstuffed with cooking equipment Charlotte had picked up from all different parts of the world, sparkled cleanly around them. None of this was to William's credit, who had been rather useless and consumed by his grief, for he was being haunted by that damned golden wood of the yellowwood that flowed through every room in the house.

William could not escape it.

He plopped himself down opposite Leila, who reminded him painfully of her mother as she sat at the table eating her porridge with a book larger than her propped open in front of her as she ate haphazardly, occasionally missing her mouth and dropping porridge into her lap.

Each time this happened, Duffy would scold her, put her spoon down and wipe the mess away with the cloth she kept tucked in her apron, followed by a swab of the child's mouth. After around the third or fourth time, William found his temper had run short, or perhaps he just needed an excuse to leave — he stood up abruptly, wiped his mouth and shot Duffy a stern look that he knew would achieve exactly what he needed it to in that instant, which was to quell any thoughts of stopping his storm out. But before he left, he paused in the doorway and said, "It does no good to scold her for being inattentive while allowing her to read at the table." Which was the most he had said in about a fortnight?

"Where are you going?" Duffy demanded of him.

"To get my mother from the harbour."

He strode steadily out into the day, not swaying on the top step and squinting into that fucking yellow light, but rather keeping his eyes down and walking with purpose — although he was still quite drunk. A buzz that should subside in about an hour or two — he'd fix that problem before long.

There was no time to waste, however, and it was a ten-hour hike to the harbour and he'd better get started if he was going to be there when her ship came in.

As he reached the wooden garden gate, the scent hit him as the breeze rustled the many blades of grass which spread as velvet over the endless rolling hills. It all just became too much for him. It was that damn golden light, carried through on the golden blades of grass this time of year — especially, and the sudden, blindingly sweet scent of the jasmine that lay lazily across the stone wall, which Charlotte herself had cared for and shaped into what appeared as a sprinkling of snow all along the eastern side of the bulky garden.

To the world, it may seem that the scent had knocked the sense from the drunken man, because he stood there with his hand on the half-open gate, in danger of letting the chickens out to the veldt, as though a bolt of lightning had shot through the top of his skull and welded his feet to the stamped down soil beneath his worn-out looking boots. A dishevelled, drunken mess.

The wind picked up over the hills and swept over him, giving him quite a substantial push. William took the reminder to get going. She was probably on the docks right now, waiting for him. "All right, darling" he muttered under his breath, turning to leave, "I'm coming."

And opening the sturdy wooden gate a fraction, he stepped out of his garden on the hill — and walked the path down through the valley into town. During the five-hour walk, he had to stop twice to find the stream as he stupidly refused to bring any water with him. It wasn't so bad on the whole, once he moved closer to the coast, the volume of trees greatly increased and he was fortunate enough to be bathed in shade after the third hour of his hike to the trading store where he fished out what he hadn't spent yesterday and paid for some sherry. Scooping the four jugs from the countertop, he growled grumpily at Serge, the mute trader, "Not one word, Serge!" Before William stalked out of the store, uncorking his first and headed straight for the beach.

He guzzled the first in less than an hour and stumbled clumsily and drunkenly along the coast. Feeling the familiar pangs of devastation settle about him, William buried his three remaining bottles of sherry, shielding them from the sun, which beat down on his burning skin. Before he knew it, he was standing knee-deep in the ocean, staring out onto the horizon for approaching ships.

Far off to his right, he watched dock workers hastily loading and unloading a handsome metal ship which William had never seen before and he stood hastily as he caught sight of what appeared to be passengers disembarking.

Clumsily, he stumbled out of the waves, almost forgetting why he was there in the first place. Moving up the beach to the docks, he took up his usual seat atop a stack of crates that never seemed to get packed onto any leaving ship. Intently, William studied face after face of the disembarking passengers, turning to chitchat with companions, scowling at dock workers and natives — but not one of them held the mischief and romance of Charlotte's face...

William raised himself dejectedly to return to his sherry when the slightest flash of a familiar blue dress caught his eye.

Gracefully, the poised woman disembarked and strode down the dock, and he found himself watching her, a hope blooming cruelly in his chest as he did.

His wishes, however, were immediately dashed as she removed the bright and wide sun hat from her head to reveal cascading blond locks which billowed in the sea breeze.

Seconds later, the blond woman on the docks squinted at him across the way through the blinding sunlight, placing her hand above her brow to block out the sun. For a few moments, the two stared at one another before she moved to give way to an older woman who had kicked up a fuss and appeared to be begging a barrel-chested man behind her to accompany her onto the docks.

The man in turn grabbed onto the bright red fox fur around the old woman's shoulders. Snorting with derisive laughter, William watched as the man choked her out for a few moments — before she managed to yank herself free, where she stumbled and toppled backwards into the water, feet over shoulders.

Behind the spectacle, his eyes found the familiar disapproving leer of Eleanore Bennet, his mother and he suddenly recalled through the drunken fog in his brain, why he was there.

But he didn't want to see her, didn't feel ready for the cold stare or the lack of compassion... William felt a sudden urge to hide his face, a burning in his legs to run.

Sneakily, as she was distracted with her luggage and before she could spot him, William turned heel and strode back down to the beach where he found the boots he had used to mark the spot of his buried treasure and dug up one of the three jugs.

Then he found a comfortable seat. Shifting the sand slightly, he took his position and sat peering out at the endless horizon, imagining Charlotte on the deck of some nameless ship which barely touched the waves.

Gulping down his second bottle of sherry for the day, William lay back, sprawled across the sand beneath the vast open sky allowing the sun to beat down on him. Intent upon a drunken beach nap, he saved the other two bottles to drink on his way home at around midnight when he usually wakes. Perhaps he'd catch another ship coming in today — these docks teemed cruelly...

Around two hours later, William begrudgingly dug up his last two remaining bottles of sherry. He had been unpleasantly woken by the cold water which had splashed uncaringly over his sleeping form.

Sodden and coughing, William sat up and looked at the iron-coloured waves which rose and broke, rolling dangerously close now.

Perhaps he could let the waves take him, and let them carry him to wherever Charlotte was...

When he carried himself back through that garden gate in the early hours of the following morning, somewhat sozzled — the tricky west wind sought again to disquiet him. For as he reached again for that sturdy garden gate, it came rustling through that jasmine and caressed his dirty unkempt face just as Charlotte's fingertips had grazed against his skin so gently countless times before.

Grief reared up with that cantankerous wind and struck him with a heavy blow in his gut. He recalled her beautifully precise hands dancing over the vines as though she were playing an elegant golden harp instead of cutting and shaping a stubborn creeper. Shaky Charlotte, they had called her — when he had first laid eyes on her. William had managed to ease her trembling, however, he had held her hands in his own and felt the love bloom through her palms. Quite suddenly, he found that he could not breathe the scent in anymore — it was driving him insane!

Frozen and swaying, he stood for so long that he roused suspicion. Before Duffy could get to the front door with her candle, slippers sliding off of her shuffling feet, he had lost his grasp. Wrenching and ripping the jasmine from the stone wall with horrible crunching tearing noises, he roused the chickens and screamed at the sky, at Charlotte for leaving him.

"Stop, Abelumbi!" Duffy ran to him, "Stop!" Dropping her candle, she raised her hands to grab him up into one of her soothing hugs.

"Get out of it!" He turned on her, yanking the bulk of the plant from the wall with his cut-up left fist and he let it fall to the ground before, seething — he turned to pull another.

"WILLIAM!" She yanked his arms away, knowing he'd regret this once the drink had worn off! Knowing that he didn't want the jasmine gone; it was his wife, their beautiful Charlotte whom he yearned for. He was inconsolable and out of control and Duffy's protests fell on deaf ears as William yanked fist full after fist full of Charlotte's prized pink jasmine from the wall.

"Look at what you've done to her flowers!" Duffy sobbed, "Look at what you're doing to her daughter."

Glancing up, William looked at Leila's bedroom window on the second landing. Sure enough, there she stood in her cotton night dress, looking down upon him as though he were some feral stranger and he found that he could not glance upon her face for longer than a few seconds. Storming inside, he shut the door behind him leaving Duffy to follow him in angrily. She stood at the foot of the stairs on the first landing, glaring up at him and called to his retreating back, "Your mother arrived this evening, William!"

But William merely waved her off and kept climbing with an absent-minded and avoidant, "Good, good."

He was at the top of the stairs now, standing right beneath the trapdoor which led up into the observatory. Without a word, he took two steps to his right before she impatiently strode up those stairs saying, "William, you left here to go to the docks — why weren't you there to meet her?"

Dismissively, he waved her off for he was now in the same spot he started his day in, and would start tomorrow in as well. And sensing her form still lurking there, he sighed impatiently and said, "I was at the docks, all day - I must have missed her."

Then he laid down on the floor of the second landing directly beneath the line which Charlotte's feet once paced, a floor above in the observatory.

"Charlotte's ship still hasn't come in." He sighed tiredly and in madness, kicking off his boots.

"Soon, though, Duffy," William told her yawning thickly, and added heavily, with a tone of reassurance, "Our girl will be home, soon." Before he slipped off to an immediate and deep sleep.

Chapter Two

Nobody really enjoyed sharing a tent as a workspace and William was no exception. Conditions were cramped and crowded with not much in the way of air flow. This left tempers running hot and patience wearing thin. Despite his complaints to the Fund that having a woman in his research area would come into conflict with his vows as a priest of the catholic church, the Fund had curbed his application for a new workspace for the fifth and final time, with a large red stamp warning him off from ever applying again.

"Out here, you're a scientist my good chap," Professor Harper barked at him in frustration one sweltering evening while he dabbed at the continuous stream of sweat that flowed off his top lip like a waterfall in place of his usually white and bristly moustache.

He was currently shaving his face to survive the intense summer heat that coupled so torturously with the coastal humidity and stood before William, quite patchy and hilarious looking as he barked at the boy to get over himself and work with the woman.

"She's really quite brilliant, you know." He grumbled, turning back to look in the shiny metal tray he was using as a mirror, "Anyway," he chuckled, "you'd never know you were working with a woman — the mouth on her."

"Am I to take it that my resignation has been accepted?" William stood stiffly, readying himself for a good storm off.

Harper eyed him through the makeshift mirror before he heaved a great sigh and nodded, saying, "There aren't any spaces to spare, I'm afraid." Though his tone had fallen flat, as though he had finally reserved himself to what he knew was coming.

Just as predicted, William didn't wait to hear more. He turned and strode from that tent, stooping smoothly to exit with the full intention of packing his things and returning to England - at once!

Over three months, William had grown increasingly more exasperated that his complaints fell on deaf ears. More to it, his constant complaints had drawn quite a wedge between him and his colleagues. He had stretched out and used every chain of command he could think of, finally being left with no choice but to threaten his resignation.

Bitter resentment bubbled through him as he stalked back to the lab and flung the flaps aside, positively fuming that she had again closed them instead of letting the natural light and air circulate.

It was sweltering!

Charlotte wore the heat exceptionally well. In fact, the sweat running down her temples made the stray hairs that escaped her bun along her temples curl, accentuating her high cheekbones and the heat made her cheeks rouge in a manner most ladies pinched to achieve. He bristled at her, annoyed that she didn't bother looking up at him. Instead, her eyes stayed glued to the task at hand, as she was bent over a fragment of a broken stone tablet, examining it as though she could spot something her colleagues could not. Her arrogance annoyed him, and at the depths of his mind, where he kept all his secrets, he knew that arrogance was not the correct term to use for what Charlotte was. She was brilliant, and he knew it — and so did the Fund. They had chosen Charlotte over him.

If he was being truly honest with himself, something he had not done since the day his feet carried him from that party, it was this truth that irked him the most.

He fully intended to fight with her about the entrance being closed, and the heat and the light, yet again... However, when he opened his mouth, different words tumbled from his lips,

"You're better liked than I am." He said.

"I am." She sighed with a dull impatience, still not looking up.

"You're better than I am." It took a lot for William to admit this, and the weight carried into his throat, for his voice was quite strained when he said this.

She didn't respond immediately — he half-expected sarcasm from her as her eyes had left their task at his words and flicked up to his face. Finally, with a rather peculiar expression playing across her fine features, she straightened and stepped around her workbench. There was a moment of swollen silence as the heat hung on the air before she spoke softly through the distance between them, "And that bothers you?"

She was bristling for an argument, now squinting as a strip of golden light was thrown across her face when she stepped around her workspace, and he was suddenly hit with a strange — yet familiar feeling.

"You bother me." He felt his feet carry him towards her, just as they had carried him from his home many years ago. He could not recall the sequence of events, whether he kissed her and grabbed her up — or whether he grabbed her up and kissed her, the end result was all the same. Shirts were torn off, buttons flying everywhere, lips on throats and shoulders and earlobes. She raked her fingernails gently over his shoulders as he broke his vows to the Catholic Church and drove himself to the very edge of her soul again and again, where she met him in pure and gentle ecstasy.

He hadn't quite realised he was awake until his brain started registering the yellowwood ceiling above him. And before he knew it, he was sobbing. It had felt so real — he wanted it to be real. He wanted to feel her soft skin give beneath his fingers — to feel the soft, milky flesh mould to his grip as their bodies danced. The desire had become an ache. William spent his days and nights staring up at the golden wood — which transported him so jarringly to memories of Charlotte. His desperation to see her — touch her, to love her, became madness tantalisingly near to beyond control. He walked a fine edge and fully understood his thinking to be irrational — and yet, he could not veer from the path. It was a compulsion, far beyond his control.

That golden light tortured him to delirium. William had touched it — basked in its warm embrace, and now that it was gone — the world was cold and barren, and he held no love for it. Nor a desire to be in it without Charlotte.

Duffy and Langa could step into their shared role as godparents to Leila. He could stop damaging her. It was becoming so tempting...

Duffy's sing-song voice carried in a low, gentle lull from the kitchen, where his ears registered something out of the norm from their usual mornings as a hangover clubbed his brain from the floor that he used as both bed and pillow.

"Go wake your father, child." She ushered the little girl towards the landing, where he regretted hearing her little footsteps pause on the first step. She was afraid to look at him, and the shame and guilt bubbled into his throat as Duffy's words ripped through his mind as his actions of the early morning came flooding back with a burning sting to his hands. Raising them to the light, he winced as he took in the cut-up state of his palms and closely examined a particularly deep gash seated, quite painfully between the webbing of his left thumb and forefinger.

He didn't want to look at Leila's face. Instead, he faced the piano in the corner, seemingly studying the back wall. Again, he was painfully reminded of Charlotte's presence in this house as his eyes took in the half-painted mural of a kingfisher on a reed.

He felt sick. But Leila was coming up the stairs, and he'd given her quite enough to be getting on with this morning. So, he swallowed the hangover, churning his stomach, and turned to face her with an overly misplaced smile. She flinched backwards a few steps, and his smile turned to a grimace before he dropped it all together.

Leila's tone was flat and completely lacking in any respect she had ever had for him as a father, "Duffy says breakfasts ready."

His heart sank. The word, "Father," seems to have gone out the window... Yes! He could see it in her expression... When hurt, she held her jaw just as Charlotte had, and averted her eyes just the same. He knew that it could be days — maybe weeks. And, feeling the sudden need to reach out to her, he extended his arm. William wanted to hold his daughter and apologise. But she turned from him and walked back down the stairs, not looking at her father nor lingering any longer than needed.

It took everything in him to step forward, and when he reached the top of the landing, he paused and looked up the ladder to the trapdoor above that led into the Observatory. He had not been up there since he tracked Raul down at the Iron Pig... The day his world came crashing down.

The thought of not seeing her up there, pacing a hole through the yellowwood floor, squeezed at his throat and threatened to choke the life out of him until he found himself running down the stairs like a child frightened by the dark behind him.

He was prepared for, and awaited Duffy's verbal redress — he'd sooner face it than look at that empty study...

But when his feet found the floor on the bottom landing, his ears jarred at the voice carrying through the kitchen.

"Sit up girl!" Barked a voice that he dreaded to hear.

Rolling his eyes, he traipsed into the kitchen, as Duffy smiled her beautifully full smile. She and Leila sat side by side across the table from his mother, Eleanor Bennet. Duffy looked up at him and shot him a warm smile as though he hadn't acted the fool just hours ago, and he believed her. Nothing short of that could have carried him to sit with his mother whose glare now directed itself at him. Humming as always in her smooth velvety voice, Duffy wished him a genuine, "Good Morning!"

And she dished him up a steaming bowl of porridge before sitting back down, where she further added butter and honey for good measure.

As Eleanor watched this all unfold, William watched her thin eyebrows disappear further up her forehead until they were in danger of disappearing into her hairline. Choosing to let her stew and come out with it rather, he shot her a polite nod, and offered a rather flat, "Mother," in greeting. This was not a visit by his invitation, but rather by her insistence.

Picking up the heavy clay mug, William sipped the bitter coffee Duffy grew and roasted in the back garden, near Charlotte's bathtub. Eleanore continued to glare at him sitting at the opposite end of his own kitchen table. Strategically - he folded first, sighing impatiently at her, "For god's sake Mother!"

Her words formed in her disapproving gaze before they could even befall her tight-lipped mouth, and he had to fight the sudden urge to laugh as she gave the impression of someone sucking on a lemon rind, but he braced himself nonetheless.

"William!" She began in tones of admonishment, not bothering to greet her son whom she had not seen for over ten years. True to form, Eleanore was quicker to admonish than she ever could be to affection. For she had witnessed something so morally unacceptable — so ethically horrendous that any greetings or pleasantries needed to be swept aside.

Clutching at her chest, she shot him a stern look and waved her finger in Duffy's direction, "But this is quite unbecoming!"

Choosing to butter his toast, rather than give her the courtesy of an immediate answer, he shot Duffy a warm smile whilst nodding his head in the direction of the doorway, indicating that she should take Leila and leave — immediately. He let them clear out while he took his time to chew, maintaining a calm demeanour. This was crucial when dealing with Eleanore Bennet. A bloodhound who could sniff out any weaknesses.

Once he had swallowed and sipped his morning coffee, he fixed her with a square sort of glare, challenging her to come out with it,

"What is unbecoming, Eleanore?"

In a sour silence, Eleanore stared at him, her grown son, and he could see the calculations taking place between her ears. Asserting his authority within his house, William purposefully let slip a flicker of impatience, barking at her in a commanding tone never before used on Eleanore Bennet, "Out with it, then!"

"What kind of home are you giving my granddaughter, William?" Eleanore was quick on the draw, not mincing her words, "Seating the help at the table to dine with you?" She clucked her tongue in disappointment, and it was his turn to raise his eyebrows.

"Duffy is not the help," he corrected her in a chipped tone, "she is Charlotte's dear friend, a treasured historian and a world-renowned field scientist, far more qualified than myself."

"Anyway," He added, taking a deep sip of the bitter coffee, "that kind of thinking is not welcome in this house." It was quite odd. This would be the first time he had ever engaged with his mother on equal grounds, as adults.

For a split second — he thought he saw a glimmer of pride strike her iris and wrench the corners of her mouth, but it passed so suddenly that his eyes could not capture and analyse.

With a stiff nod, Eleanore conceded and offered an apology, completely taking William by surprise, for it was not like Eleanore to admit defeat like this. But she was playing the long game and allowed him a few moments of shocked silence before she moved on to her next grievance, "I saw the state you returned to the house in this morning, passed out drunk on the second landing like some common slob-"

"You took my room." He protested quite lamely and just like that! She had found the chink in his armour and loomed over him, making him feel like a child again and crumbling his calm facade immediately. For she was ultimately his mother. But she was not here to harm him, cold as a codfish, Eleanore had real difficulty showing affection. Instead, she loved in a language of actions and service.

"I took your guest bedroom," Eleanore stepped to the window to look out at the golden hills beyond the stone wall. She used gentle tones with him. A softness that he could only ever recall her adopting at his sick bed when he was hit with whooping cough and his prospects looked bleak.

"This place is beautiful."

He didn't respond. Instead, he began to choke on the lump that formed in his throat, anytime he sensed someone was about to mention Charlotte.

"You two have built quite the life for yourselves." Eleanore turned to gaze sympathetically at her drowning son, a full-grown man, a father and widower like herself. A widower locked in the earliest stages of choking even these many months after the fact.

Staring morosely at the table, William wished her away. He didn't want to speak about such matters with her, she had been most disapproving of his love for Charlotte, "Ill-fated," she had called it...

He had to fight the sudden urge to scoff at the bitter irony of it, but he could not look up at her.

He felt disquieted when Eleanore adopted a maternal warmth, for she usually employed a rather cold and callous demeanour having married for her father's political gain.

"I realise," She began again in tones of unnatural gentleness, "I hadn't been very kind to Charlotte, and I regret that." She nodded approval at her own statement, and went on, "I can see that it has torn you quite apart."

At these words, he looked up at her, eyes brimming with the loss he felt constantly cutting away at his chest and lungs so that breathing hurt. He didn't need to nod his head in confirmation, wholly screaming behind his eyes at her that he was in the worst pain of his life.

Eleanore seemed to take a few moments to steady herself for what must be said, and she looked out into those vast open landscapes once more before she turned to him, and offered a sad smile, "The life of a barrister is filled with much less death and decay."

But William was a quiet man, and barristers get paid to speak. He exercised this fact by remaining silent, though returning her morose smile with his own. Keeping to the theme of uncharacteristically maternal warmth, Eleanore reached across the small space between where she stood and where he sat. Pushing a stray hair from his face and back into place offhandedly, she mumbled, "I knew a love like that when I was a girl."

And sitting back down at the table opposite him, she sighed, "I don't think you shall ever recover."

They sat in that kitchen in contented silence for a few short minutes. The most peace he had felt in months, mind you.

But what needed to be said, had better be said now for she would be travelling back to the harbour that day...

Steadying herself, Eleanore looked her broken son full in the face and made her request, for she knew that if she demanded, or commanded he would react exactly as he always had.

"I would like to take Leila back to London with me," She laid it out quite plainly, but offered further reassurance by gently adding, "For a short stay of course."

Through a suddenly dry mouth, William gently pleaded, "Mum, I can't send her away."

And it was his turn to stand and look out of the window, "This is the only home she's ever known, and we didn't raise her to fit into that society. The plan was always to raise her here." Eleanore offered him an understanding nod, and she said, "A few months at most."

Standing to face him, Eleanore reached out and took his hand, "Let your heart break without it spilling all over her."

Chapter Three

It was not an easy decision.

But, given that he had drunkenly spewed himself all over the place for the past three months... And that Leila would no longer look at him, address him as "Father," or speak to him at all — beyond what Duffy enforced.

"I can't send her on a boat Mother!" William reasoned, but found himself falling off, unable to complete his protest, "Not with how..."

And despite Eleanore's assurances that she would never let harm befall the girl she doted on from so far away - William still could not grant his permission and stood resolute, leaving that table without further entertaining the folly.

Bitter and angry, he was fully intent upon stalking out into that garden to tell Duffy off for causing this entire debacle. It was, after all, she who insisted he write to his mother in the first place, alongside the letter she practically forced him to write to Catherine Nicholson, Charlotte's mother. But as he reached the front door, peering momentarily through the glass panes that sat comfortably in the yellowwood, he spotted the two digging in the garden but a loud and sudden thud upstairs froze him in his tracks, hand glued the doorknob.

Something whooshed past his left cheek and rustled his hair, and as he turned his back against the door, he could have sworn that he heard frantic words brush past his ear, "Send her!"

"I have tried to be kind to you!"

Eleanore came stomping through from the kitchen, where she left her maternal warmth, "But let me be quite frank." She stopped walking just in front of the landing and pointed through the glass panes past his right shoulder, "You have not been a comfort to that child."

"Do me a favour," He shot at her sarcastically, as he opened the door, "and pick a tone, will you?"

Turning and opening the front door, he strode down the front steps and into the garden towards his daughter and Duffy. The two were in the veggie patch, bent over the carrots, poking sticks into the soil to gently coax out any weeds that may have sprouted since their last attack on those well-kept beds.

Nothing, but the conversation such as the one he overheard entirely on accident, could have persuaded him to send Leila off to England with his mother.

"I do hope he lets me go, I'd much like to see London." Leila's sweet little voice carried to him on the wind, and though he could pick up the warm tones Duffy used in her response, the words seemed lost in the distance as she faced the opposite direction.

Hours later, he walked Leila back to the harbour while she and Eleanore chattered excitedly about all the fun to be had when they reached London. William made a small spectacle of himself while attempting to state some ground rules, for he would not have Leila turned into Charlotte's worst nightmare by having those wife classes shoved down her throat!

"You have to swear it to me, Mother!" He had stopped the wagon altogether at this point, "Charlotte was very clear on the type of woman she wanted to raise."

Eleanore, who had seconds before been sharing a chuckle with her granddaughter and merely offering to teach the girl to sew, stared at him, completely bewildered at the sudden intensity of his demeanour.

"Please," He begged her breathlessly, needing her to recognise him as her son, desperate for maternal warmth and needing her to recognise his need, "don't cross this."

For a few seconds, Eleanore searched his eyes before she sat back and said with a stiff nod, "No finishing school, but I can teach her." She smiled imploringly at him, "Just as something to do, you know — it rains so often." He smiled at the compromise and nodded his thanks before wordlessly turning and leading the horse down the lazy road to the harbour, over and around the many rolling hills.

Around five hours into the ten-hour walk, Leila poked her sweaty little head up in her seat, where previously she had been slumped over and halfway to dozing off...

She made no noise, pointing quite frantically off into a nearby thicket. Eleanore seemed to grasp the child's wordless communication without hassle, for she looked immediately in the direction of Leila's tiny pointing finger.

William turned and startled the metallic blue kingfisher, Charlotte's favourite bird, and Leila shot him a scathing look to make his breathing hitch painfully in his throat.

"Oh, be kind to your father, girl!" Eleanore nudged her gently, "He's lost a great deal." But he didn't look up this time, Leila had averted her eye so many times now that he knew better than to expect her to look at him. He didn't know how to apologise to her, nor did he want to admit that looking at her was deeply painful to him too — for he could see Charlotte reflected back at him.

"That was Mummy's favourite bird!" She sulked childishly in protest, "He scared it away."

"Birds scare easily to stay alive, Leila." Eleanore was no stranger to stubborn children, her son had seen to it that he got his own way in everything he did. Unlike William and more to her mother's fashion, Leila adopted new perspectives with apparent ease. Behind a crinkled brow, she looked to the empty bush, and then to the back of her father's head, thinking hard. But it was difficult for Leila to forgive his falling apart when she needed him the most. His unravelling before her cast horrid scars on her childhood and what had once been her paradise — her home, now exploded with his incoherent screaming as he lost his mind to the loss that consumed him.

"He's quite worried about you, you know." Eleanore nudged again and shot her an encouraging smile, "He's worried about putting you on a boat, in case you have too much fun with me and never want to come back!" This raised a chuckle from the pair of them and Leila looked to her father thoughtfully once more. She sidestepped her own pained perspective and understood finally that he couldn't help how it hurt. Her own chest ached hard every time she remembered her mother.

Frowning, Leila called softly over the breeze in a sweet and swollen tone, "I will come home soon, Father."

When he turned to glance back at her, it was through the tears in his eyes. The kingfisher, like Leila, was far too forgiving.

William spotted the handsome fellow in a nearby honey suckle, and he appeared to follow them all the way to the docks — where, chirping his distinct song, he flew off, skirting the ocean breeze...

To William's surprise, they were not to embark on one of the more modern steamships, but rather a sailing ship.

"Much safer!" Eleanore told him with a gruff nod and patted his arm, "Tried and tested!"

She preferred anything that wasn't still in its infancy. And while this meant more time on the ocean, it did leave less room for other technical catastrophes. William found himself nodding his agreement. Leila in turn jumped onto him. Finally wrapping her arms around her father for the first time since he had broken the terrible news of her mother's watery demise. Not wanting to let go, William squeezed her tightly and told her he would miss her before she jumped down and ran excitedly up the docks to get a better look at their ship. Completely fearless and absolutely beaming every time she looked at him now.

He watched her frolic a few moments, filled with bittersweet feelings and listening to Eleanore's assurances that she would guard the little girl with her life before he began to unload their packed luggage for the crew to take and load up before he walked them to the gangplank where a short and fat first mate ushered them rather impatiently along.

"We've got weather coming in, I'm afraid." He told them, cutting their goodbyes short, "Got to get out of the bay right quick!" And he moved on to the next group of people, too, saying a rather teary goodbye.

And just like that, he was waving her off... His girl. The last reason for breathing, and against the ill feelings that swirled in his heart amidst the black of grief, he smiled and kept waving until they were dots in the distance, and he stood on that dock alone...

Rather than wasting a trip into town with an empty wagon, William decided to stop by the trading post before heading back to the observatory. He bought barley and oats for sowing. He bought horse feed and more sherry, rum and gin to lose himself in.

He also stocked up on tobacco for Duffy, baking powder, yeast flour and sugar as the tradesman stared at him mutely from behind his countertop, while William loaded it all up. Popping back in briefly to pay, he laid his coins out across the ashen wooden counter and shot the tradesman a surly, "Don't thank me, Serge." Before he stepped out into the blinding sun and patted the horse called Silk.

Feeling that Silk could do with a refresher before they set off back up on the long journey home, he directed her to drink at the trough old Tom used to toss overly drunk patrons who stopped paying into at night. He stopped to dip in quickly at the Iron Pig for a drink and a late lunch. Perhaps more than one drink...

Silk knew the way home, and he'd be riding atop the wagon all the way back, after all.

He placed his order with Tom and turned to look around while he waited for his sorghum beer. Spotting Raul lurking in the corner and looking rather dejected behind his own large flagon, William felt his feet carry him to the man who had watched Charlotte take her last breaths.

"Got something on your mind, Raul?" He asked the dampened sailor, who flinched at his sudden appearance and squinted back up at him.

"What?" He grumbled, "Oh, ya." The old sea dog bristled then seemed to sag, as though he were deflating.

And just as William took the seat on the stool opposite him, Tom plopped a fresh and still fizzing tankard down in front of him. Momentarily, he seemed to hesitate, opening his mouth to ask something but seemed to think better of it, for he shut his mouth — shook his head, and stormed off back to the bar muttering about circuses and monkeys. Raul seemed to stare right through him before reserving himself to something as he took a deep breath and said, "Knew Charlotte right from the first ship she jumped." He looked William in the eye before asking, "She ever tell you that?"

He racked his brain for a few seconds before shaking his head, but his gaze never left the old sea dog's bloodshot blue eyes as the old man nodded and heaved a great wheezy cough before he leaned over to extract his pipe from his pocket where he then began stuffing it.

William sipped deeply from his glass while Raul puffed pensively on his pipe for a few moments before he got a fine ember burning. Turning his sights to the cottage pane facade behind him at the horse still drinking deeply from the trough outside, he spoke unblinking, "I lied to you, lad."

With a snap of electricity in the air, Raul's eyes met Williams as he went on with a rasping crackle, "I couldn't bear to watch ye comb those beaches for bits of 'er any longer and so I told you what I hadn't seen."

Sitting back, Raul puffed pensively on the acrid-smelling pipe, begging him to understand.

Evidently, the message had been received. William stiffened like a board, placed his beer heavily on the table in front of him, and raised himself slowly from his stool.

For a few moments, he stared Raul in the eye, searching, before he walked out, dropping his money on the bar. He didn't climb atop the wagon, but instead mounted Silk cleanly and left immediately for the observatory without waiting for his food, he couldn't eat anyway, flighted as he was.

He had to tell Duffy! He needed to pour over those maps! Leila would be gone for months! He could set off to find her himself. He'd rent a small dingy and row the damn thing himself if needs be!

Hardly daring to believe it, he pushed Silk as he had never pushed her before, keeping a fast pace the entire journey home up the hills and down. So much so that he needed to stop twice to lift the sacks of grain back onto the wagon as the horse moved quick enough that a small rock caused a significant bump and would periodically throw items from it. They moved with haste and seemed to bring the weather with them as heavy grey clouds loomed up behind him. Eventually, the winds pushed them over him. The birds warned of an impending storm as the air swelled and grew quiet.

He could smell the rain building and urged Silk to move faster. The last thing he wanted was to be caught in the rain in the dark. The mist began to swirl and thicken as they moved higher into the hills.

Squinting up and trying to see the sky, he felt the wind blast him, as seconds later, two fat little raindrops hit him square in the face. They were coming up over the last hill by the time the clouds had blocked out every bit of light from the sky, leaving Silk to wander the path by feel and memory as he urged her on. The sky began to throw great rumbling threats at him as seconds later — it all lit up with the first clap of lightning.

Panicked, Silk broke into a gallop, as William held tight to the reigns hearing a couple of bottles roll off the wagon and smash on the path behind him. He came up the hill at a speed, grateful to see lights burning in all windows, except the circular observatory on top of their house. William guided Silk straight into her shed and out of the rain, wagon included and hopped off the moment she had come to a complete stop. With shaking hands, he immediately loosened the buckles binding her to the wagon before he turned and ran out of the shed, shutting both doors behind him and jogging to the back door of the house that he built for Charlotte.

The back door always seemed to hitch when it rained.

William suspected water was getting in somewhere to cause the thing to swell, though he had never quite gotten around to investigating the problem. Wrenching the door open with an almighty wooden screech, William stepped out of the pouring rain, dripping all over the kitchen floor and expecting to be told off by Duffy. But when he moved from room to room, calling to her, it was to find the place quite abandoned.

She had filled up all the lamps and lit the place up so that he didn't come home to the dark... Just the lonely.

He found the scrawled note on his nightstand from Duffy, sending him love and letting him know that she would be spending a few days with Langa on the neighbouring hill to the East. Sighing heavily, William crumpled the note and headed back downstairs, and out through the front door, where he braved the rains for his booze.

Chapter Four

Stratigraphy was a far reach from what William's father had envisioned for him, and he noted the disappointment etched in every line of the late Nigel Bennet's face, but he could not walk away from a life like this.

For one thing, his interests were peaked when out on Mount Snowdon. He first learned to respect a mountain. Beforehand, his London-locked mind could never have comprehended how vast the landscape could be. He was a young lad, from a tiny world of townhouses and terraces. For another, Eleanore only had one child as was absolutely necessary and so William had not grown up with any siblings to play with and found, in his later years, that he deeply enjoyed the sense of camaraderie that coupled with this very tactile and interesting career.

He loved the mountains so much, in fact, that he put in for a position at a Swiss church, even though he didn't know a word of German. In fact, it was his arguably limited knowledge of French that saw him get the position, but it had been close and he tested the church's patience even further by underdelivering on his sermons and being unavailable as he spent so much time on the Alps.

That unsustainable setup did not last more than a few months. However, during his time in the mountains, William met and befriended a lot of scientists, explorers and madmen. Some of them were part of an exploration fund and urged him to put in an application to join them in Palestine.

"If they say no, just come anyway!" Isaac had joked, while they faced their death in bad weather at high altitude. He managed nine more climbs with Isaac before the mountains claimed him, and the catholic church had sent him eight rejection letters thus far.

With Isaac's passing, William reached a point where he was fully prepared to leave the church for this pursuit. But they seemingly had developed their own interests in Palestine. Finally, his ninth application was accepted without his resignation, and they sent him on a comfortable journey across the seas.

His journey to Ashkelon had been so comfortable, in fact, that once he arrived, it was quite a stark contrast. For one thing, it was hot, and the humidity walloped him in the lungs. For another, it was loud. His guide pulled him by the jacket through the hustle and bustle as they made their way up to some wagons and horses before his luggage was launched rather unceremoniously into a wagon piled with bags of rice. The guide gabbled at him in what he vaguely recognised as Turkish and began pushing him and urging him towards the wagons, where he confusedly turned and climbed up. This seemed to please the man who smiled and nodded his balding head at William and began walking alongside the horse.

The journey to his tent was so comically short that he could have easily walked it himself without being shunted onto that wagon. It only took about half an hour from the port. During this time, he looked around to watch the many tents and excavation sites they passed, each surrounded by scientists and labourers working to achieve some degree of discovery and understanding.

William's task was to document each new layer of soil dug up and label the strata before sending the samples to the Oxford Geological Institute. In next to no time, William managed to form strong working friendships with all of the great minds of the camp. All but one of the archaeologists...

One could argue that it was her late arrival (and annoying ease to fit in) that irked him. But Charlotte played cards and swore like a sailor, much to the delight of their fellow scientists. She also drank and smoked like one of them. On the whole, he knew that ultimately Charlotte irked him because despite her hands that shook, and her frankly unfeminine ways, she achieved everything with apparent ease and meticulous professionalism.

Everything except what he needed her to achieve.

"Hold it still!" He barked at her in frustration for the second time in five minutes as she held up the fragment in question, "How can I be expected to examine it if you can't hold it still?"

From his perspective, this was a completely reasonable argument to make. However, Charlotte closed her fist around the fragment, shot him a scathing look and told him he was more than welcome to hold the bloody thing up himself to look at before she stomped off.

This had been the first anger anyone had ever seen in Charlotte, and the other chaps felt that it was frankly warranted as they got along with Charlotte just fine. Even telling William on more than a few occasions to stop being such a prat.

It had been a fragment of bone. Not human, though they never really managed to figure out precisely what it may have belonged to. The mystery had evolved to a silly guessing game and the two delighted themselves in drawing pictures of lunatic-looking creatures, all of which sat in a neat pile atop one of the many bookshelves in the observatory. The fragment rested permanently atop a pile of Charlotte's favourite folk tales when not being used to prop open maps.

If you were to hold that fragment of bone up and drop it directly down through the floor, it would land exactly where William laid his head night after night, right between the eyes and take him out of his misery. He had drunk all his stores and spent three weeks on a bender. And now his liver hated him, and his heart still ached for Charlotte. Desperately, William stared up at that yellowwood ceiling and watched, in his mind's eye, Charlotte pace back and forth above him in front of that pile of books crowned with their fragment.

Rudely, Edward stepped over him and walked down the stairs to the bottom landing, where he yawned and stomped sleepily into the kitchen as though this were his own home.

William lay on his back, staring at that ceiling forcing himself to take no notice until he distinctly heard that useless lump sit at the table, and sigh loudly before calling out, "Duffy!"

Silence. Then, "Duffy! Breakfast!"

The Nicholsons, who incidentally were the very same people who had made such a spectacle of themselves on the docks, turned up three days into what became a full-scale cyclone. Sodden and shaking, they claimed to know nothing about Charlotte's passing, and they didn't seem too saddened by the news either. Arguably, that may have been because Charlotte's family had wandered the mist and storms for three whole days with nothing to eat or drink before Langa and Duffy found them dangerously near the cliffs.

William had spent the day falling down drunk in the rain and throwing Charlotte's things into the wild waters of Blood Rock when he stumbled into the kitchen and found them standing around the dining table, wet and shaking. He let them stay in his guest bedrooms, forcing Catherine and Mary to share one while giving Edward the other.

For three weeks, while William lay catatonic on that second landing floor, the Nicholsons ran over Duffy, treating her like a maid and their personal servant. Understandably, Duffy took to hiding in her bedroom when not caring for William - who had again slipped into a deep depression.

Doctor Duffy Duduzile Dlamini was a loyal friend — undeserving of the ill-treatment received at the hands of these admittedly horrible people.

Mary was the eldest of the three Nicholson children, then there was Charlotte who followed two years behind her, and Edward who followed five years later. In the small bits that William caught in his catatonic state, the whole world appeared to revolve around Edward, as Catherine saw to it that Mary ran circles around him. Always ensuring his comfort.

"Duffy?" Edward called again and again from downstairs, leaving William grinding his teeth in annoyance until he could take no more.

Irritated, he sat up. Marching stiffly down the stairs, he loomed in the doorway catching Edward completely off guard.

"Duffy is not a servant, you are free to make your own eggs."

Edward blinked at him stupidly for a few seconds before it dawned on him that he had crossed some line. Absently, he smiled at William and uttered an embarrassed, "Right." Before standing and setting about rather vaguely to look for the items he needed to make himself eggs and had clearly never done such a thing before, much less in a stranger's kitchen in a foreign land.

By his understanding, Edward had been a small boy when their father had tragically and quite suddenly passed on a rainy Sunday afternoon. He hadn't learned very much of anything. Charlotte, who had been gazing out of her window trying to see the stars past the lights in London, watched her father fall. It was this reason that she gave William, an explanation of her pull to her grandfather's library.

Initially, Charlotte had held no interest in books. The simple truth of the matter was that the library was located on the highest floor of the Nicholson Manor. In short, it was the only room whose windows didn't haunt Charlotte with images of her father's struggling form plummeting right past her in a blur.

A small girl too shaken by what she had seen to ever look out any of the windows beyond that top floor, she spent such vast amounts of time shut up and away from the sun that her skin grew sallow. And with little else to do, she began to flip through the pages of the many books that surrounded her igniting the spark in what became the brilliant mind of Charlotte Nicholson, now Bennet.

Feeling it would be rather unkind to allow the man to flounder for much longer, William sighed and stepped into the kitchen pointing out the cast iron skillet hanging from a hook right next to the wood stove.

Ears burning scarlet, Edward snatched it up off the hook, and placed it on the stove before he turned hopefully back to William, who offered an encouraging smile and pointed out the butter and eggs on the yellowwood countertop, also next to the stove...

"Salts right next to the eggs," he chuckled as he turned around and headed back up the stairs to his spot on the second landing, feeling that Edward could figure things out from there.

As he reached the top landing, however, he was met with what sounded like a loud explosion but turned out to be Catherine's good morning greeting.

Behind Catherine, a short and dumpy woman stood her tired-looking daughter, fresh-faced, though frankly over her mother and he shot her an understanding smile.

"Dear William!" Catherine's screechy fish wife's voice set a cacophony about the air, "You're finally up!" It was not unlike a cat yowling in the dead of night or nails on a chalkboard...

Behind her, Mary smiled apologetically. Quite haggard and tired-looking, she leaned against the ladder which led up to the observatory and he felt distinctly hot under the collar. As though a great spotlight had suddenly cast its blinding light down upon him.

Catherine went on like a canon, "I do hope you slept well?"

Before he could smile and lie about how well he slept, she swept on, speaking over him in a forced accent, "It was ever so kind of you to take us in, dead of night like that!"

And, simpering with a girlish sort of giggle, she added, "We'd been lost out three days!"

Most bizarrely, Catherine offered a hearty laugh to this before flicking her fan open with a snap where, lightly she fanned herself and fluttered her eyelashes at him.

"Yes," William offered as a rather vague response, trying to mask how strange he found her behaviour to be...

"Well," he said awkwardly, turning on the spot as he searched for something to say in response. Thankfully, he needn't search very long as the awkward moment was interrupted by the click of Duffy's bedroom door behind Catherine, and both Nicholson women whirled around to face her.

Duffy, in turn, offered them all an overly friendly smile and chipper morning greetings before she strode between Catherine and William, whose face broke into a grin when he saw her.

"And where are you going all dressed up like that?" He was smiling pleasantly at her, taking in the whole effect of her beautiful yellow dress as she swept past him, holding a wide, fancy-looking sun hat in her delicate hands. The colour complimented Duffy's skin much like the golden light that flowed through this home, and which haunted William so cruelly.

Duffy shot him a coy smile and told him of a picnic basket awaiting her on the next hill over, and he returned her smile mischievously, "Oh?" He prodded rather more playful than he had been in months.

"And who will be on that blanket beside you?"

Duffy giggled, quite unlike herself, and fixed her hair in the mirror behind him before she hastened down the stairs to the first landing without finishing his conversation with the unwanted guests. Knowing the answer, he followed her down and chuckling, teasingly, he asked her again. He wanted to hear her say it out loud, for Langa was his best friend, and, by this point, he had chased Duffy for well over a decade and a half.

She paused at the door and smiled up at him, now placing the sweeping sunhat that matched her pretty dress quite nicely atop her tamed hair which she had secured and tucked neatly using pins adorned with pearls.

"You look beautiful," He told her at the door, holding it open for her to exit into the morning sun, "May I walk you?"

And to this, she chuckled and elbowed him saying, "Nosy!" Though she was quite overjoyed to see him sober and walking around. Deciding to indulge him, Duffy smiled coyly at him, "If you must know," she stepped lightly toward the sturdy wooden gate, "— has been asking me for three weeks now, and I've run out of reasons for turning him down."

She left him at the garden gate and made her way up the road, apparently opting to save her leather high-heeled boots. She took the long way around rather than cutting cleanly across veldt and hills. William only watched her leave for a moment or two before chaos again seemed to explode within that previously quiet home.

Edward, it seems, could not handle the rest from there...

Somehow, he managed to set the curtains on fire in the kitchen. How he achieved this was a feat beyond William's imagination, as the curtains were located on the complete opposite side of the kitchen from the wood-stove. Nonetheless, he doused the flaming curtains using a nearby vase and turned to face Edward who was standing in the centre of the kitchen. He stared vacantly around for a few seconds, before he blinked and said, "I'm so sorry, I'm barely awake."

Like a blast leaving a canon, Catherine came bustling into the kitchen as though he had survived some catastrophic ordeal. Habitually, Mary seemed to sweep in and take over the preparation of Edward's breakfast, not uttering a single word, but very clearly irritated as Catherine lamented the dangers her poor boy was put in and how brave he was for fighting a fire.

Scoffing, William left the three of them in the kitchen. Fully intent upon returning to his spot on the second landing, out of habit more than anything. But when he reached the top step of the second landing and looked up as usual at the trap door in the ceiling, he was shaken to find it wide open.

Trembling, he stepped nearer to the ladder.

Peering through the portal entrance into the observatory that had stayed shut up and vacant since the day Charlotte's ship was supposed to come in, his breath hitched as he heard a dull thudding along the wood above him. It was as though someone was running along the planks right at the door above him!

Horror coursed through him as he braced himself for the runner to come barreling through the door above him. Instead, he felt a faint tap on his shoulder. Heart pounding in his throat, he flipped around to see Mary standing behind him on the top step of the landing, needing to get past him. Seemingly on her way back to the guest bedroom she currently occupied with her mother to escape the din, now echoing through the entire house out of the kitchen.

He looked up once more at the open portal above him and called to her retreating back, as she had now managed to squeeze past him and stood in the doorway to the passage beyond the second landing, "Did any of you open this?"

Momentarily, her hazel eyes, so similar to Charlotte's, flicked up confusedly to the open door in the ceiling and she uttered a surprised, "No," with eyebrows raised, but didn't say anything further. Quite ludicrously, William found that he did not believe her, and he told her quite stiffly, "No one is to go up there!"

Wide-eyed, Mary nodded her head, eyes never leaving his own and driving him mad as she tried to further assure him that nobody had gone up there, but he climbed up that ladder and shut the door wordlessly with a snap, not looking at her further. Marching back downstairs, he turned heel and headed out the front door, presumably back out to the recovering jasmine hedge, which he had taken to standing near when he wasn't lying on the floor of the second landing.

Chapter Five

Charlotte's hair billowed in the wind in front of him. Tresses, the colour of molten espresso, dazzled him in golden flecks each time she caught the sun's adoration. In his memory, she laughed deeply from her throat as she turned her face back to him.

He couldn't recall what he had said to make her laugh so freely, but her laughter sat in his memory as crystal clear as the water cascading down the smoothed-down rocks of the secret spring the two lovers happened upon while exploring the surrounding areas of their chosen point of construction for their observatory.

William felt his breath taken by the wind as the red rocks contrasted so jarringly against the pristine sky. So red were the rocks, in fact, that Charlotte staked the name and called it Blood Rock.

Quite the hidden gem. Only found by following the sounds of water down what appeared at first glance a perilous sheer drop. However, further down the slope — rather closer to the edge than any life-loving person would be comfortable with — skirts a narrow path bordered with ferns and wildflowers around the mountainous hill.

Cautiously, they followed the path, which eventually opened up to a shallow pool that flowed gently off the cliff edge.

A gentleman, he had merely stripped off his boots and socks and rolled up his trousers to the knee before carefully wading into the pool. Charlotte, on the other hand, stripped off entirely, boots, socks, trousers, blouse and underclothes all tossed to the nearby rocks as she ran naked, and laughing, straight past William - who had his back facing to her and was examining the rich iron rock face beneath the calm and gentle cascading water.

Horrified, William watched her laughing face disappear over the cliff edge, quite unsure he had really seen her speed past him like that. Seconds later, he heaved a great sigh of relief as his ears registered a loud splash.

"Are you insane!" He yelled over the cliff edge at her, less than five metres below him, and she swam naked and laughing to the edge of the deep pool — which she had scouted whilst stripping down.

"William?" Edwards' face loomed into view, cutting across the golden wood ceiling he had been staring at once again. William didn't answer but rather looked at Edward, who was kneeling above him for some reason.

But when Edward merely continued staring down at him from his kneeling position, William shot him an exacerbated, "What?"

He appeared to have forgotten his reasoning for bothering William, who was currently in his usual spot, in his usual state...

"Oh, right!" Edward smiled abashedly as he suddenly recalled what he was there for, "Me an' Mary was wonderin,"'

William sat up, forcing Edward backwards as he spoke, "If there's anyfing to do out here?"

As he said this, a thick bead of sweat dripped down his left temple. In an instant, William's mind seemed to register how sweltering the day had grown as the sun beat down on him through the window in Leila's bedroom.

Sitting up, and swaying drunkenly, he turned to see Mary standing nervously out of sight. Halfway down the stairs, she peaked her blond head up to watch the interaction and he suspected that she was too nervous to ask him this herself. Perhaps Mary was afraid he would snap at her again... He didn't think Edward was clever enough to feel boredom.

Blood Rock was nearest and deepest for swimming, but he somehow felt that taking Charlotte's family there would be a terrible injustice to her. Taking something precious from her and gifting it to them, though they were undeserving.

Instead, he took them to the caves.

The insides of some of the caves held pools that were just deep enough for light swimming and wallowing away from the intense heat of the day. The two younger Nicholson's were actually rather enjoyable when separated from Catherine, who opted rather to stay at the sweltering house, to complain about the heat and lose herself in her embroidery.

"Are you still horribly cross with me?" Mary asked him from the water, as he sat quietly in deep thought, dipping his feet.

"No," he mused quietly, not looking up from his feet in the water.

Truthfully, he wanted them to return to England, so that he could get going. He didn't quite understand fully why he chose not to share this hope with them. Charlotte is, after all, their sister and daughter. However, his memory could never recall Charlotte ever speaking fondly of them. In fact, his memory could never recall Charlotte speaking of them much at all, aside from basic details surrounding her father's death and the horror surrounding her escape.

"Why did your mother punish Charlotte, the way she did?" William asked the question out of thin air, after minutes of being lost in silent thought. Mary, who had since climbed out of the water, was wetting her finger and using it to paint spirals on the flat rock. She lay spread out and drying, propped up on her elbows, as her vague smile immediately slipped from her face. Nervously, she glanced around for her brother, who had taken one of William's bottles of rum outside.

The half-drunk bottle in his own grasp — hung rather loosely from his left hand, which was propped up on bent knee as he lazily dangled his right in the cool water.

No answer came immediately from Mary, and she appeared to be searching his face before a sad sort of smile curled her lips. And, glancing off to the near distance, she said, "Because Charlotte wasn't like me."

Sipping and losing himself in thought for a moment, William winced slightly as the liquid burned seductively down his throat.

Then he pointed toward the mouth entrance of the cave and quietly said, "Nor is he."

Mary raised herself to sit with her knees to her chest, reaching out and prompting William to hand her the bottle, which he surprisingly did without question.

Then she took a deep gulp, and wincing, she coughed and told him, "He is not a she." And he mouthed a long and silent "OH" in understanding.

For the first time since their arrival, Mary let her tears out, and they shook her hands to the point where he was reminded painfully of Charlotte as she sipped. She did look quite a bit like Charlotte if he thought about it — which he tried not to do... Same brows, and the same nose but her jawline, lips, and face shape were entirely different, more slender.

"Truth be told, I admired her courage." Mary wiped her tears away, as though annoyed at her loss of control. Quickly, she regained her composure by taking a deep gulp of rum before she sighed and said, "Some of us were a bit more prepared to let bits of ourselves be cut away."

Leaning over to hand him back the bottle, Mary him in the eye. Adding in a suddenly coy tone with a strange far-off sort of smile playing across her lips, "But not Charlotte."

At that moment, he reached over and took the bottle back as Edward stumbled back through the cave entrance, and he realised, by the light quality, the lateness of the hour. Completely distracted, he didn't even notice Mary's fingers trace over his own gently as she returned his bottle.

"We should be leaving." He told them both, lifting his foot from the water and standing to head back. The trouble was that drunk and wet feet don't mix at all well with smooth stone. Gracefully, William flew through the air and into the water, where he landed with a loud splash.

Completely infuriated that he would need to make the long, half-hour walk back up the hill wet, he waded to the edge, wiping his face. When he lifted his right foot and stepped out of the pool, however, there was an odd and burning tightness around the joint between his foot and its largest toe.

"Mate," Edward said dully, pointing down at his foot.

His body would not allow him to apply the pressure he needed to step out of the water. Awkwardly, he was left standing there with his toe sticking out at the wrong angle and hopping on one leg in the waist-deep water, "Your toe is broken." Edward finished his thought dully.

Mary took a few seconds to take the sight in. Completely horrified, she stood up quickly from her perch and held out her arms to help him climb from the water. Once she had got him up and he was sitting on the side, she stood up and marched over to her brother. Snatching the other bottle of rum from his ham-like fist, she marched it over to William, who took several steadying gulps as she knelt in front of his deformed foot.

The pain had begun to set in, at this point and, he could not flex his toes, much less walk on the foot.

"I'm going to set it right." Mary breathed, looking him wildly in the eye, as a faint shimmer of Charlotte appeared in her before him. Nodding his head gruffly, and taking yet another strong gulp from that bottle, he braced himself for what must come as Mary thumbed over her shoulder, "He can carry you back."

She moved smoothly, wrapped her spindly fingers around the toe in question and yanked upwards. Instantly, there was a dull and painful pop, followed by a horrendous burning and stinging sensation as the thing began to swell.

But he could suddenly move his toes, and — despite the horrifyingly intense pain... The relief was unimaginable.

"Put that in the cold water," She urged him gently, "it'll help with the bruising and the swelling."

She helped him lower his injured foot into the cool pond of the cave.

"Where'd you learn to do that?" William made sure to avert his eyes, another flash of Charlotte, and he was sure to be undone... Wincing slightly, he let his foot sit in the cold water for a while. Mary glanced nervously over her shoulder at Edward, who stood half in, half out of the cave, unsure about what to do with himself.

He understood that she could not tell him what he wanted to know, but rather suspected that Charlotte was not the only daughter in the Nicholson household that secretly consumed literature in her grandfather's study.

And he further suspected that Mary had probably been far more secretive about it, as Charlotte's nature had always been quite on the nose.

It felt a bit humiliating, to be carried by another man up the hill.

Once they reached the plateau, he gruffly fought for his dignity by insisting they let him walk. The path back from here was relatively flat. He had walked it with a twisted ankle many times — this was no different.

Though he had to admit, it was distinctly more painful to walk on injured toes.

Nonetheless, he lumbered back home and winced his way up those stairs where he again took in the infuriating sight of an open portal door leading up to the observatory where Charlotte spent most of her time. Furious and in an immense amount of pain, he stalked up the passageway towards his and Charlotte's bedroom where he flung the door open, not wanting to look at the empty bed. He took a few seconds to get himself a set of clean and dry clothes from the wardrobe, while he grumbled about giving Catherine a piece of his mind when he noticed it.

The dent in her pillow.

And the more he looked — the more he could see blatant clues of a disturbance in the room. He had not touched the bed since Charlotte's ship was supposed to come in. The bright burned amber-coloured quilt was thrown back with a noticeable body dent in the coverlet.

Moments ticked by before his brain whirred back into motion. Forgetting momentarily, the pain in his foot, William turned to leave before recalling his injury, and he pulled his foot back from the pain which lifted an audible grunt from his lips.

Once he managed to make it downstairs, into the kitchen, the sumptuous aroma of whatever Duffy was serving up in a steaming pot smacked him square in the face. She was midway through serving the rice coupled with the beautiful curry in the steaming pot in the middle of the table while Catherine shot looks at her turned back.

Perhaps his intense emotions stemmed from his suspicion that Catherine had laid in his bed, or perhaps they overflowed because he had addressed her attitude towards Duffy more times than he should have needed to.

Regardless, he decided to say something, and apparently looked quite mad, standing there, still dripping in the doorway, "Is there a problem with the food you are being served as a guest in this house, Catherine?"

Caught off guard and under a spotlight, Catherine choked mildly on air as she blustered an embarrassed, "N-no!"

Staring Catherine squarely in the eye from across the table, William spoke to Duffy, "We'll be getting back to research next week, Duffy." he breathed, not looking away from Catherine, "And you are not to extend your kindness to this woman any further." As he said this, he pointed at Catherine, who gazed open-mouthed at him from across the table, quite frankly flabbergasted.

But Duffy wasn't his pawn and nor would she allow herself to be used as such. Shooting him a scathing look, she asked him, "Anything else, Baas?" Before sitting huffily at her own spot at the table, which Catherine would have blatantly preferred her not to have.

Immediately, he turned back to Catherine and slyly jostled her.

"Go on, Catherine," he said, "tell me why you lay in my bed."

Mary lifted her head up and shot her mother a questioning look, but Catherine merely continued to sit there as though she had a hot spotlight beating down on her, rendering her silent and gulping like a codfish.

"Matter of fact..." William rubbed his hands together, elbows on the table resting on either side of his plate, "Why don't you tell me what I really want to know," he said, "something you've been skating around since you got here."

The resentment echoed through his voice as he watched her sniff in disapproval, pick up her cutlery and start picking at the delicious meal Duffy poured effort into.

"What is it you'd like to know, dear William?" She looked up at him, forcing a sweet smile and placing a small forkful of rabbit into her mouth.

"Why did you really come here?" He asked her, leaning forward across the table, "What are you looking for in that study?" He nodded his head backwards in the direction of the staircase. Breathlessly, Catherine stared silently back at him, looking like a cornered rat.

Chapter Six

She lay across his chest peacefully. Breathing deeply, the sighs and warbles of sleep while William, too, lay dozing in the intense coastal heat.

"I'm leaving the church!" He had come to her that day and stood in the tent breathless as though he had sprinted a mile.

Charlotte did not immediately react. Instead, she looked pensively up at him for a few moments, searching his face, for he had never expressed a desire to leave the church up until that moment. The strong silence left him a little embarrassed at his own enthusiasm as, carefully, Charlotte placed her dusting brush back into the tray of tools to her left. Then she removed her head mirror and wiped her sweaty brow before rising neatly from her stool.

Tantalisingly, Charlotte walked smoothly around her desk with her face still dirty from the dust on the wind. And when she was within arms reach, William pulled her to him and felt her give off heat like a furnace.

"Is this what you want?" She asked him, just millimetres from his lips.

This was all that he wanted, and he crossed the small distance and kissed her fiercely, answering with action.

Hours later, William gently roused her sleeping form. In his memory, she was warm, and soft from deep sleep when he pulled her to him and placed kisses along the bridge of her nose.

"Will you marry me?"

Sitting up groggily, Charlotte rubbed her eyes and took a few moments to study his face.

A few moments to understand that William adored her, just as she adored him. In that beautiful moment, Charlotte smiled sweetly at him, kissed him and whispered, "Let's elope."

"Out with it, Catherine." He spoke calmly to her from across the table while Catherine betrayed not even a hint of mildest indignation at his sudden accusatory tone.

"I wrote you myself to tell you..." He could not finish this sentence, and Catherine capitalised on that fact, immediately snapping her fingers at Mary, who sat up at attention like a trained dog.

"Get him some wine!" She barked at her daughter, "Can't you see the poor chap is battling?"

"No!" William spoke firmly, but his word, it seemed, had held no weight. Duffy looked over at him before she sighed in annoyance and spoke up sternly, "Answer the question!"

She had her fork halfway between her plate and her mouth, and slammed it down, "Stop plying him with drink and answer his question!"

There was a nasty silence. The game was quite clearly up, and Catherine stared back at Duffy through eyes the size of saucers while Edward frowned at his mother in deep thought... Or at least, effort.

Mary, who had been halfway to the wine cupboard in the entrance hall, flinched at the clattering sound and halted immediately in her tracks, quite unsure what to do.

"Go on," Catherine told her daughter, trying her hand. With a nervous nod, Mary turned back to the cupboard before Duffy pointed her finger at her and said, "Don't move girl!" Now staring Catherine full in the face and rising from her seat. Catherine too, began to rise from her seat before William quietly and calmly looked over to her and said, "Sit down, Catherine."

"I'll be upstairs in the study, working," Duffy told him, storming off and not wanting to be around these people who vexed her day in and day out as though she were their servant, and without thinking — he nodded his head in agreement and acknowledgement as she passed by him. Duffy exited that room so fast that she created a small gust of wind that rumpled her skirts.

"I'm perfectly capable of fetching my own drinks, Mum." He nodded politely at Mary and employed formal tones of sarcasm. Mary, who flushed bright red, returned to her seat, eyes averted.

And when she was finally seated, he looked into each and every single one of their faces as though he were trying to pull their thoughts through their eyes. First Edward, to his immediate right, was still looking between William and his mother, unsure what to do. Though William detected a distinct threat in his posture. Next, he took in Mary, who breathed quite deeply through parted lips, as though gasping quietly and inaudibly, eyes wide and terrified. And finally, to

Catherine, who fought hard to keep her face impassive.

"Why were you in my bed?" William demanded of her.

Catherine opened her mouth, shut it — then opened it again before she finally chirped out imploringly that she hadn't.

"You didn't?" William asked her sarcastically, "Then why is my bed disturbed?" Mary looked round to her mother with a questioning look and Catherine looked over to her, willing her to believe, as she breathed, "I didn't." Now looking down at the plate of food in front of her, she waited a few moments before lifting her head and locking eyes with William, "How am I to climb a ladder?"

Catherine used logic and reason, adopting imploring tones that never met her eyes, which stayed locked to Williams until she drew her gaze away and looked again to Mary.

"Are you calling me a liar, Catherine?" William began to raise his voice. He felt frustrated and with the Nicholsons in every room of his house, he was finding it distinctly difficult to breathe. As though their presence sucked the air from the atmosphere in his world.

"I'm not calling you anything, dear." Catherine scooped up a fork full of curry and continued to smile her maddeningly sweet smile. At that moment, William suddenly understood what it must have felt like to try and reason with Catherine as a child about hopes and dreams only to have her smiling back and chewing her food on her front teeth.

"I'm sick of the games, Catherine." He told her, steadying himself.

"There are no games, dear."

This was maddening, and he slammed his fist down on the table next to his bowl of food.

Edward rose from his seat with a sudden ferocity that William readied himself for an onslaught. Instead, Catherine raised her finger, and sternly told her overgrown lump of a son, "Sit down or leave, Edward!"

Who chose the latter and left the table. Seconds later, they heard the front door slam shut as Edward stomped down the front steps and out into the garden.

Mary looked from William's face to Catherine's.

"I didn't do it." Catherine told her, straight-faced and bold, "Go look for yourself, if you harbour any doubts." And Mary, looking her mother square in the eye, raised herself from her seat — before she, too, left the table. This left William to stare angrily across the table at Catherine as they heard the wooden thunk of Mary moving in haste up the stairs, much the same fashion as Duffy had done earlier.

In the wake of the silence, William had the sudden realisation that he had drunk his fill of these people. The bad weather had passed, and he wanted them out of his house. "Ultimately, it matters not."

He told Catherine, raising himself from the table, not swaying in the slightest for he was stone-cold sober, "I'll have the wagon readied for you to leave at first light tomorrow."

Limping off up the stairs to the second landing, William looked up at the portal door and called to Duffy. Perplexed, she opened the door and peered down at him through the ceiling, "That fast?"

And despite himself, he chortled and shook his head, "No, they'll be leaving in the morning," then, "come down, would you?"

Duffy shot back without a moment's hesitation, "Come up."

But William paused and fidgeted uncomfortably with his fingers. He hadn't been up there since the day Charlotte was supposed to come home. The room scared him for some reason, though he'd never admit such a childish thing to anyone.

"I'm not coming down there until they're gone." Although she was being quite firm, Duffy spoke with a warmth and a smile that he desperately needed at that moment. It was only that which could have raised his foot and placed it upon the first step of that ladder leading up to the study where Charlotte spent most of her time.

Before he knew it, she was stepping back to allow him the space to clamber through the trap door on the observatory floor, and he breathed deeply the overwhelming smell of books and jasmine. The sunlight dazzled them in reddish light, now beginning to set in the late afternoon.

They stood together, looking around the room so devoid of Charlotte that it brought them both to tears. Though it held the same contents and captured the same light, Charlotte's absence echoed through the many shelves of books and treasures and relics and scrolls.

He found himself staring at the thread-bare rug, in which she had carved out a worn-out strip with her relentless pacing as she read book after book in absolute peace. Duffy looked over to him, smiling serenely and rather sadly. She said, "It'll never be the same without her." And, wiped his eyes off the tears that had begun to flow like a river down each cheek.

"I can't thank you enough." He told her, standing in that circular study. The two people who loved Charlotte most in the world. Shaking her head, Duffy held both of his hands in her own. He understood enough and received the gesture as warmly as it was given.

And when he looked at her, she was smiling rather strangely at him, as though dread had trickled through the minuscule gaps between the floorboards beneath which he had been lying and staring up at for four months solid now.

"Just a little longer," William whispered, wanting to reassure her, "then we can go find Charlotte." At this, Duffy did the slightest of double takes before looking at him rather pensively for a few short seconds.

Hesitantly, and carefully, Duffy spoke in a firm tone, telling him the truth he needed, but did not want to hear, "Charlotte's gone, William."

"No," He told her, now smiling widely as if this was all just some silly sort of joke, "Raul told me the truth of it! She lives!"

He fully expected her to jump for joy at this revelation, but she did not. Instead, she dropped his hands, crossed her arms in front of her and squirmed rather uncomfortably as she searched his face.

"William," She breathed finally, gazing at him with nothing but heartbreak in her eyes, "come back to us."

He blinked at her, confused, but just as he was about to ask her what she was talking about, Mary called him from the second landing below. When he walked over to the portal door to peer down at her, she frowned up at him before saying, "She's telling you the truth."

"You're still leaving in the morning." He told her, not caring anymore and shutting the portal door to leave them to their packing.

"Don't you think you should deal with that?" Duffy asked him, quite shocked at his response. Though the rudeness was warranted, it was quite unlike for William to behave this way, and it clearly made her nervous. Obviously, she had no desire to continue their previous conversation, and undertones of dread began to needle at him the longer he looked at her.

"No," he said stubbornly, glancing over at the door on the floor of the steadily darkening room, "they're leaving." He wanted to reassure her, he wanted to apologise. But instead, he ended his sentence with a well-meaning, though obviously tense, smile.

When she spoke next, it was in a forced calm, "When last did you sleep, William?" As she asked him this, she held the back of her hand to his forehead, as though checking for illness. But he smiled and took her hand in his own, as he told her "I'm perfectly fine."

"Answer the question." She was being rather stern with him, and his smile dropped off quite easily because it didn't belong.

"A while." He sighed, finally and she frowned at him, inwardly making the confirmations, though outwardly she nodded stiffly and responded immediately, "To bed then!"

Pointing at the door, and foot tapping like an irritated mother, Duffy marched him to the portal and opened it to see Mary still standing down there.

When she saw this, she appeared to lose all patience and barked, as she made her way down the ladder, "What do you want, girl?" And hopping down the last few steps she added, "Why are you standing here?"

"Erm," She tried to look around Duffy to William, a fact not missed by Duffy who gave a stern look, hands on her hips as she barked at Mary, "You can speak with me."

And when Mary still didn't answer but merely continued to point weakly towards William, Duffy offered her a kind smile, gently took her hand and urged her back up the passageway where William could hear her explain in a bright and patronising voice that "Master of the house said that you would be leaving in the morning!" Mary hummed and hawed her way down the passage next to Duffy, who plainly was taking no prisoners or letting anyone get a word in edgeways, "I'm afraid he's had a long couple of months," Duffy simply simpered in her most British accent, pulling a chuckle from William, who still stood upstairs and alone in that observatory, "and you have so much to pack before I take you back to town tomorrow."

"You, take us?" Catherine could be heard butting in, clearly unpleasantly surprised, "Yes!" Duffy exclaimed in response as though her question was a silly one asked by children, "And I'll see you safely onto the docks myself!"

When she walked back beneath the portal to get downstairs, she shot William a celebratory smile from below.

William didn't come down from the observatory that night.

For one thing, it hurt his foot intensely getting up and for another, he'd had quite enough of their guests who didn't seem at all perturbed by the untimely passing of his beautiful Charlotte. Their dinners all remained abandoned at the table for the flies as the sun settled for the evening and brought the frogs and crickets out of hiding.

From his vantage point, he watched bats swooping in and out of view, feasting on moths and beetles that lazily surfed the warm wind currents that swept over their hill.

Respect was rather lacking with this lot, who loudly complained about being ejected so unceremoniously until pretty much every single candle in the house was snuffed out by a smiling Duffy who reminded everyone in a singsong voice that they had an early start and should really get to sleep.

And with that, William settled himself down on the cosy lounging chair Charlotte had imported from France, a genuine smile playing across his tired face for the first time since Charlotte's ship was supposed to come in.

Chapter Seven

Charlotte had a copper bath shipped in from India upon the construction of the observatory. He installed for her outside in the veldt in a spot she picked out. On occasion, Charlotte would boil up pots upon pots of water, and add some soapwort with a sprinkling of aloe flowers and salt. With the sun shining down on her naked skin, Charlotte could soak for well over an hour with her nose buried in a book. She looked like heaven.

Now and again, William would saunter up the hill to sit with her in the breeze of the late afternoons as she bathed. At times he would read to her. He adored these moments of contactless intimacy shared between the two and smiled at the memory of the milky water and how soft her skin felt afterwards.

The ceiling of the observatory was really a pattern of shapes depicting the different stone calendars Charlotte had seen all over the world. These left a reminiscence of star constellations above him even after the sun came up and the hot tears dripped down the sides of his face, pooling into his ears. Wiping his face, and not knowing how long he had been crying, William raised himself to look around the empty study. Devoid of Charlotte, and now, Duffy. William had stared at that ceiling, just as he had been staring at the ceiling beneath him those many nights, recalling every second he spent with Charlotte, every precious memory, every laugh, every sigh.

But up here...

"It's like she's here." Duffy whispered to him in the early hours of the morning, when she popped up to the observatory to let him know that all unwelcome house guests would be leaving shortly, "Would you like to come down and say your goodbyes?" This was met with a sarcastic scoff to which she returned the brightest toothy grin and called out loudly over her shoulder, "No! You cannot come down William!" And she turned back to smile at him before retreating out of that portal door in the floor of the Observatory, she called in the same pitch. "No arguments! I don't like the look of that foot!" And she shot him a wink, before leaving him to the silence of the house he built for Charlotte, while her family left practically kicking and screaming.

Immediately, as he heard the sturdy garden gate click shut outside, he climbed, wincing painfully, down the ladder. Then, he limped down the stairs and spent hours scrubbing their presence from his and Charlotte's home. Only once the place was to Charlotte's standards of cleanliness, did he reward himself with a cold bottle of gin as he returned to the observatory. The sun sat level with the clear and polished glass which filled nearly every wall of the rounded room, and limping to his lounging chair, he had to place his hand in front of his face to block out the blinding rays.

The relentless sun raised the exhausted man from his seat, and he limped carefully to the large brass telescope he and Charlotte had spent so many evenings gazing through together with laughter and lovemaking. Lifting it clumsily, he shifted the telescope to the south-facing window. Peering through it, he let a chuckle escape him as he thought of their bitter and resentful expressions and wondered if they had reached the dorp yet.

They must have done — it had been hours...

He and Charlotte would use this same method to check on each other during supply runs. The memory of seeing her through that lens struck him so suddenly that it swept the air from his lungs. In a moment of delusion, he thought he'd actually caught sight of her. When he panned his telescope back to the place he thought he'd seen her standing and waving at him, all he found was an empty cliff face.

William was having a difficult time spotting the travel party. For ten minutes, he searched the hills and concentrated hard as an ominous feeling began to take hold of him. But as he stared through that lens, a tapping sound caught his attention with a snap at the opposite end of the room. Alarmed, William straightened and looked round to investigate, heart beating in his throat.

Once he moved, however, the tapping seemed to cease immediately, throwing the room to sudden silence, filling his ears with the sound of his own breathing.

For a few short moments, he listened hard and held his breath. Once he felt certain that the tapping must have been in his mind, he shrugged it off and continued his search for Charlotte's family through the polished telescope.

After around ten minutes, the idea of watching them walk away dejectedly from this vast distance seemed to lose steam. Thinking that they had probably already passed the dorp, he left the telescope. He walked vacantly around the study, looking at signs that Charlotte had once been in there.

He passed by her fiction shelf and found sea shells and a golden chain lying scattered in front of the books. Through tears, he remembered that beautifully clear day they had spent on the beach after the construction of their observatory was completed.

Trailing his hands along the dusty bookshelves, William moved around the large circular room until he reached the last shelf. This shelf held around sixteen black leather-bound journals, which he understood to be Charlotte's research. With a sudden longing to trace his fingers over her handwriting, to feel the indentation of the paper where her ink and quill had danced, he lifted the first off the shelf. Opening it at random, he began to read,

"*March 15, 1865*

Dear Diary,"

Carrying the book over to his new sleeping place, William began to read.

"*The day unfurls before me like a delicate blossom and I find that I have no desire to declare its beauty, but rather to crush it beneath my foot.*

As I sit alone, in this dimly lit study, I am compelled to commit to parchment the relentless tumult that rages within my soul. It has been mere months since I first took refuge in you, my silent and impartial confidante, and this evening, I unburden myself once more.

The world beyond your pages is a prison of unspoken expectations and while it is not categorically stated what is expected of me, I fear my education is grooming me for a life I never wanted. My dreams, once radiant stars in the night sky, have been smothered by the heavy hand of societal expectation, for I am expected to wed."

She had never told him that...

William, looked up from the book and around the room, as though searching for Charlotte to query one of the passages in her research papers. He always read her research before she sent it off. With a pang, her absence filled that room.

Shaking his head, as though dazed, William tried to remove the horrid feeling that had returned to fill him up. To himself and for comfort, he repeated the words, "She's alive!" and "We'll find her!" again and again until he felt steady enough to read on,

"In the stillness of this chamber, I find only fleeting respite — a meagre sanctuary, where I may let my true self be known, however briefly. I etch the scars of my resistance upon the parchment of my existence with each scratch of this quill.

Today, the world remains a hostile landscape, and I, a reluctant traveller on a path strewn with thorns. With a soul so heavy and burdened, I take my pen to chronicle the daily injustices and the quiet, ceaseless battle that rages within me.

Yours with fading hope,

Charlotte."

Enthralled in the mind of a young, rebellious Charlotte's pages of history, William read through the next few diary entries. Imagining the sixteen-year-old Charlotte sneaking into her grandfather's library just as she had told him she had.

"*He is old and vile,*" A later entry read, when William flipped to April fifteenth, an entire month after the first dreaded entry.

"I cannot pronounce his family name, but I needn't bother," Young Charlotte had written, "I won't be marrying him. I have decided to make myself absolutely foul — so that he may seek a bride in another more desirable young woman."

Chuckling, William flipped through a few more pages as he watched Charlotte rebel silently through the pages of her diary until around an hour later when he came upon an entry reading, "*My plans have succeeded, diary, I am free.*"

Smiling and heart swelling with pride, William held the book to his chest and slipped off into a deep, and rolling sleep.

For the first time in months, he didn't dream of Charlotte or their candle-lit laboratory. He wasn't plagued by the golden light either, for there were no dreams to disrupt this very needed rest.

Hours crept by, and sunlight swept through the library moving from its eastern sunrise to its western sunset all while his rumbling snores swept through the house, even reaching the bottom landing and bouncing off of the walls towards the kitchen as he slept the day away.

It was a few hours from midnight before he woke to that same faint tapping he had heard earlier. Sitting up, he yawned widely, feeling quite strange, as though he had been bathed in light. Stretching stiffly, William swung his legs back over the edge of the lounging chair and placed his sock-clad feet on the thread-bare Persian rug Charlotte had nearly paced a hole through.

Tap! Tap! Tap!

Rubbing his eyes tiredly, he stood up slowly and stooped to pick up the leather-bound diary, which must have fallen off of his chest at some point during the day.

Tap! Tap! Tap!

Duffy should be back by now...

He walked over to the window in front of his telescope and peered out of it into the night. It was easy to see across the moonlit hills of the midlands, with no light inside the place to blind him to the night. For a few moments, he scanned the hills intently while his stomach betrayed a hungry grumble.

Tap! Tap! Tap!

Ignoring that incessant tapping, William made his way slowly down into the kitchen on the injured foot. There wasn't much in the way of provisions, so he fixed himself a simple jam sandwich with Duffy's homemade bread. He ate slowly, hoping Duffy had the good sense to bring back more rum. It was only once he had eaten half of his sandwich that he remembered that Duffy had baked that bread for Langa over on the neighbouring hill. Feeling guilty, he stuffed the last of it into his mouth and headed back up the stairs, still wincing at the pain in his toe.

Surely Charlotte had a book on bread somewhere up there.

Once he had clambered rather clumsily through the portal door in the ceiling onto his knees on the observatory floor, he straightened, grunting audibly and began to peruse the many nonfiction books Charlotte kept. None were cookbooks.

Slightly panicking, he turned this way and that, scanning the shelves until he ended up right next to his telescope. Peeking through it at the distant road, he saw nothing but bats swooping in and out of view as the moon dazzled each blade of grass, giving the hills a slight glow of their own.

For a long time, he stood there, gazing hard at the road.

Until the tapping started up again with a slight quickening to the succession. At that moment, three things happened at once.

Just as he thought he had spotted Duffy on the distant hill, where she appeared to run into view, waving her arms at him from afar, a blue kingfisher flew directly into the window in front of him with a horrid and sickening crunch and cracking the window with an earth-shattering crash!

Flinching away, and heart pounding in his throat, William next heard the front door open and seconds later, slam shut.

He took only moments to catch his breath before he moved backwards towards the portal door in the floor, intent upon catching Duffy before she got to bed to say thanks and offer her his deepest apologies for eating her bread so thoughtlessly.

Wincing horribly, William lumbered clumsily down the ladder whilst calling out to her and checking that he hadn't, in fact, broken his injured toe, "Duffy?"

Feeling satisfied that his toe was not broken, he began to limp down the stairs vaguely as he called out to her, "Duffy, I'm so terribly sorry-,"

But it was not Duffy standing at the foot of those stairs, moving to come up.

Instead, three familiar faces stared up at him, quite as surprised to see him as he was to see them.

"Where is Duffy?" He asked them flatly, extremely annoyed that they had come back.

"You mean she isn't here?" Catherine asked him, looking perplexed and placing a foot on the bottom step. "She left us at the harbour ages and ages ago." Her children rallied beside her for support, both nodded vehemently, eyes wide as saucers.

Chapter Eight

It was William who first met Duffy.

Duduzile Dlamini, an equally fiery woman as his wife, at the time of their meeting, spoke English more eloquently than the men she was physically throwing from her makeshift tavern on the docks. She made her money dealing cards, hosting illegal gambling rings of dice and selling drinks to the dock workers and local sailors.

Duffy's tavern became a regular haunt for William and Charlotte who preferred a laugh as opposed to the petty tensions over at the Iron Pig, where the British and Dutch patrons bickered over their beers and started full-scale brawls.

It was Langa who first introduced William to Duffy.

Following a long and hot day of fishing on the beach, Langa persuaded William to stop in for a quick drink before they would take the long walk home in the dark.

"Come meet my girl," he smiled at William, who walked beside him up the beach.

"You have a girl?" William chided, nudging Langa teasingly as they walked side by side. They had lived in tents in the open field for about four months at that point and were about midway through their construction. Langa befriended William almost instantly, for he was a lonely goat herder who had lived alone in those hills since he buried his mother four years prior. Chuckling at the look on William's face, Langa shook his head and tapped his temple with a knowing smile, saying, "Not yet, but soon." As two grown men came sailing through the air in front of them.

Searching his memory for their parting words of that morning, William eyed Cathrine suspiciously, but he could not recall Duffy ever telling him where she would go once she left the Nicholsons at the docks...

Perhaps she had gone to Langa's kraal over the hill. Nonetheless, he didn't feel like dealing with the Nicholsons and asked them quite plainly, "What are you doing back here?"

Catherine opened her mouth to speak, but Mary beat her to it, "The captain said there was bad weather coming in!" She spoke hurriedly over Catherine's shoulder, for she knew that William was on the cusp of throwing them out in the dark. At that moment, she arched her eyebrows in earnest, and appeared almost identical to Charlotte, sweeping the air from William's lungs.

"Right." He mumbled, faking a steadiness that surprised himself, "And did he say when to come back?"

All three shook their heads, no.

"Fine." He said with a slight bark of annoyance as he made his way down the stairs, parting the group. Turning his heel, he stalked into the kitchen, no longer noticing the pain in his toe. They heard him opening draws and rifling through their contents before his footsteps came bounding back towards them, leaving a stern thump across the stone floor — and a hard thud as he marched, with a limp, up the wooden stairs.

They watched him disappear down the passageway, where he closed and locked his and Charlotte's bedroom door. Then he stalked back up the passage — now wincing at the pain in his foot, which became more noticeable as time passed.

He stopped in front of the ladder on the second landing and peered down at them all, dislike etched in every line of his ageing face as they all stared quietly back up at him.

"You can sleep in the same rooms," he told them begrudgingly, "we will wait for the weather, and I will take you back myself." Then he turned right around and climbed up the ladder and into the observatory, shutting the trapdoor with a snap behind him. And he locked it for good measure.

Moving over to the polished yellowwood desk, which overflowed with books and maps, William lit a candle, wishing to lose himself once more in Charlotte's written inner musings. He dropped the key onto Charlotte's desk and then strode over to the shelf that held all of the leather-bound journals. Picking up the first journal, William returned to his cosy lounging chair. Carefully, he placed his candle on the side table next to the chair and away from anything that could catch fire, and then he sank into the cosy chair and curled up to read.

"April 10, 1865

Dear Diary,

Nearly a month has passed since that pivotal day when I stood my ground, and with conviction in my voice, bid farewell to the much too old man, whom I was bound to wed too young.

His departure was bitter, marked by sharp words and disappointment and though mother seems to hate me completely at this point, I feel it was a victory for my dreams, my independence.

As I reflect upon these weeks, I find myself still buoyed by a sense of liberation, as though I have broken free from my shackles. The promise of a future unburdened by that ill-fated union continues to fill me with a sensation of empowerment, a flame that I cannot extinguish, nor allow to be snuffed out.

It is with a heavy heart, dear diary, that I confess my battle to be far from finished. This evening, as the sun dips below the rooftops of London and the shadows grow long, I received news that has left my heart shattered and my spirit heavy. A diagnosis — one that I had always feared but never dared to acknowledge in this plain of existence — now hangs over me like a pall.

Hysteria, they call it. A malady that plagues women like me, those who dare to seek knowledge, independence and a life beyond these narrow confines. It is as though my dreams, once so close to fruition, have been cast aside like ash from a dying ember.

The words of the physician, spoken with detached certainty, echo in my mind. He offered no solace, no understanding, only a prescription to quiet the tumult within me. They would rather I be docile and complacent, it seems, than strive for something greater.

But, Diary, know this: I will not go quietly into the night. I shall fight with every last remaining breath that I possess. The diagnosis may cast a shadow, but I shall be a beacon of nought but defiance from henceforth.

At this moment, my happiness has been dashed upon the rocks of reality, but I shall rise, Diary, like a fabled phoenix.

Yours, with a heavy heart and spirit unbroken,

Charlotte."

When the sun next rose, pressing its golden light on William's lidded eyes, the candle had melted to nothing but a waxy puddle atop the yellowwood side table — that had now hardened enough to peel satisfyingly from the wood.

He amused himself by doing just that for a few moments before gathering the wax in his hands and collecting it all in one of the large lidded jars that Charlotte kept topping up to be reused. She kept these neatly atop the farthest shelf from the western-facing windows, the only place in the room that didn't see direct sunlight.

Once the wax was stored for reuse, he moved carefully to where his telescope stood, facing the road headed south towards the coast. Instead of glancing through the telescope in the hopes of catching sight of Duffy, William moved to examine the cracked window in front of it.

It must be quite late in the morning. The sun was already heading to its highest point in the sky, and he spotted Mary walking in the garden near the jasmine, which he noted was growing back with unnatural haste.

"You didn't cause much damage," Charlotte spoke kindly to him from behind, placing a gentle hand on his shoulder. Whipping round, and heart beating fit to burst, William scanned every inch of that circular room for a sign that she had been real. That Charlotte had really reached out and touched him.

But as he turned on the spot in the centre of the room, William understood himself to be completely alone. The isolation was magnified by the dazzling golden light as a fly buzzed somewhere against one of the windows, trying to escape the room.

But there was no escape.

William turned back and walked over to the window to look down through the cracked glass at Mary, who was now leaning with her elbows on the wooden garden gate. She appeared to be gazing unblinkingly down the widened dirt path beyond. Behind the spider webbing on that glass, William stood breathless and afraid. He had felt her hand, its warmth still radiated through his shoulder, and her voice...

He was absolutely certain he had heard her, even felt the air brush past his ear.

A soft knock on the trap door drew his attention momentarily as he stared at the spider webbing across the glass. Measurements for a replacement pane were needed — and so, ignoring the soft knocks that would interrupt him periodically, he moved around Charlotte's desk. Behind the desk, there was a massive travelling trunk, which was used to store all of Charlotte's tools. Painfully, William knelt in front of the trunk and flicked each of the two lockable latches open.

"William," Catherine called softly from the landing below through the closed door with a muffle, "you're supposed to keep that foot elevated."

Once opened, he swept aside the white linen cover cloth and fished out a tape measure from the neatly organised array of tools. Typically, William would have used his own measuring tape, however, his toolkit was in the shed out back, and he didn't feel very much like gracing the unwelcome guests with his presence just now. Lest they mistake his good manners for the welcome...

He shuddered at the thought as Cathrine called to him again from beneath the trap door on the second landing. Without saying anything, he limped back around past the door to the window. And call it petty, but he took care to step with more weight than he usually would, making it blatantly obvious and hard to miss that he was ignoring her.

Once he had the thing all measured and his required dimensions quilled onto a piece of paper from Charlotte's pile of scraps - William hobbled over to the trapdoor and stooped to unlock it. He found climbing down the ladder to be far easier and less painful than climbing up. With ease, he moved down, right past Catherine, who pounced the moment his painful left foot made contact with the second landing floor.

"William?" She implored him from the shadows in the corner where she had been lurking like the wraith she was. Any semblance of forced patience with Charlotte's family had long since fluttered away. Snapping at her, William no longer disguised his annoyance with silence, "What!" He bellowed in her face, "What do you want, Catherine?"

Refusing to believe her to be as dense as her son. How could she be so unable to take the hint that he held no desire to speak with her? With any of them for that fact...

But Catherine was relentless.

"I fear we have been terrible house guests." Her blue eyes implored him, and he shot her a look which she didn't acknowledge as she went barrelling on, "We owe you and Duffy both a huge apology and our thanks!"

Her chest heaved up and down with such rapid succession that she appeared to be panting, and he eyed her suspiciously before nodding in recognition of her apology, though still not speaking to her."Is there anything we can do to repay our gratitude?" Again, he looked into those blue eyes so alike in shape to Charlotte's, which had been hazel. But Catherine's eyes held none of the warmth that Charlottes had. Gently, he took her hand into his own as he looked into the depths of her cold blue eyes. And when he spoke it was in tones dripping in earnest, "You can leave." He told her, wiping the smile from her face as he let go of her hands gently still and turned to leave down the stairs.

"Where are you going?" Catherine suddenly demanded from the top of the staircase as Edward appeared through the kitchen and Mary opened the front door. He got the funny impression that he was being surrounded, but he brushed the thought off and silently strode past Mary, and out through the front door. Once out in the yard, the three surrounded him again, halting his progress out to the shed. There was a weird feeling about them. An urgency that did not match the situation and he eyed them all suspiciously.

"Where are you going?" Catherine's demand was met with raised eyebrows. Perplexed, William held up the piece of paper and said in a rather chipped and impatient tone, "I need to order some glass for the broken window upstairs."

Without a moment's hesitation, Edward grabbed the piece of paper from his hands, grunting, "Let me go for you!" As Catherine and Mary ushered him back inside chaotically, promising tea and cakes which they had annoyingly spent all morning on, and, no doubt, used up the last of Duffy's flour and sugar.

Annoyed, he told Mary to ask her brother to get some more before he left and handed her some money from his pocket, finally giving in to their attempts at gratitude.

Chapter Nine

William's divorce from the catholic church was a day of great significance to the young couple, who celebrated it alongside their wedding anniversary. The two had cheekily eloped the same day a year after the fact. Ensuring a laugh that would see them through to their last remaining days.

"I used to be quite respectable before I met you." William found his laughter and kissed her along her jawline. Her skin coated his as their bodies pressed together, and she let out a soft, seductive sigh that echoed off the walls as a chuckle. Like water, she moved against him and whispered, "Serves you right, getting involved with a hysterical woman."

He adored the flickering quality of light on her hair as she threw it back and danced for him, all he could do was hold on. His hands snaked up her thighs to her hips, to her waist where he held her and met her swaying with his own. Suddenly, he was not perched on the hard surface of smooth river rock but floating amidst the clouds as she breathed life into him, wrapping herself around his entire frame as he absorbed her and she, him.

Her chest, an orchard over which he had free reign, lay bared before him, heaving as Charlotte journeyed far beyond the realms of his handling. Longing to kiss her, to consume every drop of her, William reached up and pulled her to him. Gently flipping her to lie cradled in the rock beneath him as the water played gentle tunes of flowing tranquillity around them.

"I love you, Charlotte." His voice was a hoarse whisper, barely giving her the time to respond as his kisses grew in hunger for her.

William had wandered a desert his entire life, dying of thirst before he met Charlotte. The flickering light of their torches danced off her hair as he wrapped it around his right hand, longing to touch it, to feel more of her softness that she presented only to him. And as he did this, that eerie golden light, which had so cruelly plagued his world since his memory's inception, danced off of her hair and told him quite plainly that he had reached heaven's gates.

“Did you give him too much?” A faint but familiar voice echoed somewhere near and far. “No, I’m quite certain-,” an equally familiar voice responded — and Charlotte began to fade from his grasp as that golden light surrounded him, filling their cave and enveloping him as she let him go.

When he awoke in his own bed, he was alone.

Though the scent of jasmine still lingered on the empty pillow beside him. As William's brain began to wake, he registered the dip in the pillow and leapt from the bed as though it were on fire and those crisp white sheets had seared his skin. He let out a horrible gasp, frozen with his back to the wall unable to look away from his marriage bed — where Charlotte smiled and waved at him through the flames. But he blinked, and when he opened his eyes, the sheets were not charred, the fire was gone, and so was Charlotte. Terrified, William flew out of that bedroom and down the passageway, silently grappling with his unravelling mind. He marched down the stairs, seeking comfort in Duffy from his waking nightmare.

Once he reached the first landing, however, William realised the pain in his foot to be almost completely gone. He could walk without wincing, in any case, and he stood there for a few moments pondering.

"Duffy?" He called to the seemingly empty house, unsure how much time had slipped by him in his fugue state. There was a bang and clatter in the kitchen as the smell of freshly baked bread drifted by.

But upon entering the kitchen, he did not find Duffy baking a replacement loaf of bread for Langa, patiently awaiting his apology. Instead, he was hit with the smell of laundry as the two Nicholson women stood side by side with their backs to him. They stood at the stone basin scrubbing and wringing in hushed chit-chat — not noticing William until he coughed politely behind them. Mary caught sight of him first and nudged her mother on the shoulder, leaving an awkward silence in their wake.

But Catherine was never one to allow such a moment to linger.

She smiled rather breathlessly at him while frantically drying her hands on Duffy's apron.

“William!” She simpered, "It's lovely to see you up and about dear!" William did not return the smile, he felt disquieted by their presence in his house, as though they oiled the floor and time slipped by him. Keeping his face impassive and his tone flat, William asked, "Is Duffy back yet?"

They shared a look, two women, who smiled at each other, but Mary stepped forward and spoke, "You just missed her."

She, too, dried her hands on the apron she had donned, and William noted with a heavy pang that it was Charlottes, "She went to go see her fellow, over the hill there." Mary pointed vaguely in the direction beyond the back door.

"Take that off," William said gently, though the danger in his voice was unmistakable. Mary stared at him for a few seconds, eyes wide as saucers as she registered his expression and pointing finger.

Hastily, she reached back and untied the apron, eyes never leaving him, and she hung it back on the hook on the cabinet next to the stone basin.

He gave a gruff nod, turned heel and walked out of the kitchen, ignoring Catherine's offer of breakfast as she pointed weakly at the two loaves of bread cooling on the dining table.

He hadn't slept in his own bed once without Charlotte. And, shuddering at the broken habit, he marched up the stairs, with his brain full to burst. With the greatest of ease, William climbed up the ladder to the observatory, momentarily impeded by the locked trapdoor.

A fine layer of dust had formed over everything in that study, and he moved, breathing hard toward the telescope only to find the cracked window completely repaired. The more he glanced about the room, the more seemed to be out of place. Their browning bone fragment sat next to the pile of fable books, the telescope faced the wrong way, and on and on the list of things out of place grew. The trunk of tools stood open, and the rug lay askew. In fact, the only thing untouched throughout the room were the books.

Perplexed, he crept up to the desk and picked up the bone fragment to examine it. He saw no indentations, the surface remained polished as Charlotte kept it, no cracks to indicate that it had fallen from the pile. William was forced to conclude that it had been moved once again. But it could not have been the Nicholson's this time...

The door had been locked, and the key hadn't left his pocket. Not that he knew of anyway.

Carefully, he placed the bone fragment back on top of the pile of fable books that had become a sort of shrine. With his mind toiling ceaselessly about lost time and the general state of dishevelment, William moved to Charlotte's journals, once again seeking to comfort himself with his wife's hand. Taking complete advantage of the bright sunlight that swept through the windows of the circular room and cast the dust motes into glittering sparks, he curled up on that lounging chair and let his fingers glide over her words.

For days and days, he read, awaiting Duffy's return and waiting for the weather to build and break, after which he would take Charlotte's family back to the docks. But the days had been lovely, and his drink cupboard was still full. So he remained curled up on the lounging chair and flipped the pages open to where he last left off, in April of 1865.

Most mysteriously, however, the next page dated was, "November 20, 1865

Dear Diary," Charlotte's handwriting had grown increasingly less structured over the missing months as he read his wife's teenage descent into the most tumultuous time of her life.

"It has been several long, desolate months since I last set pen to paper within your confines. Time has blurred into a disorienting haze which clouds my vision as cataracts, and my once-vibrant spirit now languishes in a flickering dim.

I have returned from that abhorrent place — the asylum they deemed necessary for the treatment of my 'hysteria'. Oh, how I wish they could feel my wrath diary, the things they did to me... The memories are ceaseless screams which now echo through every chamber in my mind. The days within those wretched walls felt like an eternity, diary, and I was not told how long I would be imprisoned there. There were no visits from Mother, no letters from Mary and I was faced with the utterly devastating revelation, diary, that I have no one. I am alone in this never-ending nightmare from which I cannot escape, but I must!

The treatments, if one can call them such, were barbaric and dehumanising! They sought to quell the fire of my spirit with ice baths, restraints and the vilest concoctions meant to sedate my thoughts and I lost track of time entirely for weeks on end. My voice... My pleas for release were drowned in the clamour of desperation that rose from the countless other screaming mouths of the forsaken women who, like me, dared to dream.

I learned to smile and remain blank behind the eyes, emerging as 'cured' from that hellish abyss, to which I am determined never to return. They took something from me, Diary, and I cannot get it back. The flicker of defiance that once burned so brightly within me has been doused with cold water, replaced by an insurmountable emptiness. The weight of the stigma, the cruelty of a world that seeks to silence me presses upon my chest at every waking moment of the day, and when I dream it is of a noose around my throat.

In returning to the world outside, I have found little comfort. The world continued to turn, Mary got engaged, Mother seemed oblivious as always and Edward got that Worthington girl pregnant, it seems. Of course, Mother won't shut up about who she feels is really at fault here, and I must continue to smile and remain blank behind the eyes, barred from this study, my sanctuary. But not tonight, diary, for I have returned and I have decided.

Yours, still shaken but with mounting courage,

Charlotte."

Turning the page to lose himself in the next chronicle of Charlotte's harrowing foundation, William glanced habitually up at her desk. Out of the corner of his eye, when he glanced back down at her journal, he could have sworn he had just seen her leaning over her desk as though tracing her finger along one of her many maps of the world. Jolted, he jumped up from the lounging chair and walked cleanly across the room as the floorboards creaked beneath his weight. Creeping closer to the desk, he noted with alarm that the bone fragment had again been moved off of Charlotte's pile of fables and was now being used to prop open one of the corners of Charlotte's map of Africa. Heart beating in his throat, he stepped closer and registered the scene before him. For the first time, he noticed what fable sat atop Charlotte's shrine of fables when a warm gust of berg wind blew through the opened window and flipped the book cover open to reveal the title of Robinson Crusoe, Charlotte's favourite story.

With a shaking hand, William lifted the book and held it, feeling warmth radiate to his palms. He flipped slowly and pensively through the pages of the book that had inspired Charlotte to run.

"Being lost on a deserted island with no one around sounds like a dream come true, William!" He recalled her joking playfully while she unpacked those books from the many travelling trunks that littered the place, at the time. And smiling fondly to himself at the memory, he felt her hands move over his shoulders. This time, however, William did not flinch away in fright. Instead, his smile deepened, and he closed his eyes, leaning into the sensations of her kneading hands, massaging away the tension caused by her absence.

The desire for it to be real overwhelmed him, and he opened his eyes upon the sudden realisation that none of it was real. He stood alone in that empty study with Charlotte's favourite book in his hands.

Through the tears that welled so suddenly in his eyes, William gazed down at the desk and traced his fingertip familiarly around the coast of the southern tip of Africa. Vaguely he could recall having done so many times over these many months, trying to discern where the currents may have carried her. Again he wondered how much time had slipped by him.

Cautiously flexing his injured toe beneath him, William tested it gingerly on his full body weight, surprised to find the pain minimal at most. He walked a few paces across the thread-bare rug much as Charlotte had done what suddenly felt like aeons ago.

A soft knock on the trapdoor brought him starkly back to the present, where he had stood momentarily stationary, entranced at the scent of the jasmine drifting by in the hot air.

He turned slowly to face the door as Mary carried up a tray of drinks and eats with surprising grace. Misreading the surprised look on William's face, she shot him a sheepish grin and made a light joke of wishing to run away to join the circus as a girl.

For a few moments, Mary stood awkwardly holding the tray so tightly that her knuckles turned white before he nodded his head, indicating that she could set the tray down on the table next to the lounging chair.

With a jolt, he noticed Charlotte's diary lying on the floor, not quite recalling when he had dropped it. Stooping alarmingly quickly in front of her to grab it, Mary jumped in fright, almost toppling the bottle of rum a top of her tray. He shot her an apologetic grin and replaced the books each back in their rightful places before turning back to her, hands in pockets, still smiling politely and offering his thanks for the meal. This unnatural shift seemed to throw Mary off balance. It was becoming increasingly difficult to gauge William's moods. Nervously, she studied his smile and fidgeted before turning to pour but flinched when he barked at her to, "Leave it!"

Holding back tears, she shot him a scathing look and strode past him toward the trap door before seemingly changing her mind and turning back to face him.

"Tell me, William," she shot rather thickly at him as her tears began to cascade down rosy cheeks, "did it ever occur to you that I lost her too?"

Emotion appeared to overwhelm Mary as, without warning, she broke into fits of sobs. But he wasn't having it. He was done with the charade, and he wasn't even sure of what the charade was!

Looking her dead in the eye, he stepped forward and slowly placed frustrated emphasis on each word he spoke, "I wrote to your mother and told her what happened," he said, "I don't believe that she never received my letter." And at these words, Mary seemed to lose all remnants of patience, "Dash it all William!" She was now yelling and stepping towards him, drawing something from her pockets. "You never sent it!" She waved the parchment in his face, now slightly crumpled in her grip.

"I found it on your dresser last night when I put you to bed!" She concluded breathlessly, throwing the paper at his feet, "It would be lovely if you could stop treating us like vermin!"

"Why did you put me in that bed?" William suddenly found that his throat was dry and his hands began to shake.

"I couldn't get you up here," she told him reasonably, gesturing around the place, "you've been rather heavy on the drink as of late."

There was a few moments of silence, where William felt horrified, and where he believed her. But when he looked up to offer his deepest apologies, he suddenly found himself looking past Mary's shoulder. Standing behind Mary, a sly grin playing across her face, Charlotte whispered in a voice that carried past Mary - but one that Mary did not hear, "That's how they get you," she smiled beautifully at him through that blinding golden light, "logic and reason."

Chapter Ten

In the earliest hours of June 18, 1882, William carried a pregnant and labouring Charlotte up the carved-out and contained staircase to her metal tub. Here, Duffy frantically shovelled red-hot coals beneath the tub and Langa came up over the hill with four more buckets of water hooked over his muscular arms.

Gently, William lowered Charlotte, still clothed in his linen shirt, straight into the steaming hot water in the hopes that the heat may bring her some small semblance of comfort if not a subtle reprieve.

Surrounded by her chosen family, Charlotte laboured and contracted as William kissed her fingers, clasped in his own at the side of the tub. It pained them to see her suffer, but there was a lot of laughter and love as the four of them worked to bring Leila safely into the world.

And when the pain grew too great for Charlotte to remain in the tub, they all helped to lift her out, they all helped to dry her off, each sending intentional love through their caring hands. She shivered only a few moments as Langa peeled off the sodden shirt and wrapped her warmly and safely in his Golden Basotho blanket, passed down from his mother.

They walked with her, gently supporting her across the stone floor in the kitchen until it was time to push. William crawled up behind her and urged her to keep going where, utterly exhausted, nature progressed the birth with or without her approval. They used buckets of warm water and fed her honey treats to help fuel her efforts. But after seventeen hours of labour, the exhaustion caught up to her, and she began taking three-minute naps between contractions.

"Come on, love!" He whispered in gentle encouragement behind her ear and supported her weight as another contraction rocked her body. It was time!

With all the support of the three people who loved her most, William supporting her back and holding her hands while Langa held her legs -

Charlotte pushed with all her might. "Almost there!" Duffy urged her, readying herself for the catch, and with a golden bright smile, she laughed to the panting Charlotte, "I see brown hair!"

Clasping her fingers once more in his own, William urged her on, "One more, come on love!" Charlotte screamed in agony, willingly ripping herself open as Leila's head emerged slowly and silently.

Worryingly, she wasn't moving. Not a frown, not a breath to soothe the panicking parents. "Why isn't she crying?" William asked, terrified and Duffy clicked her tongue at him, annoyed, "Calm yourself Abelumbi!" She told him, adding a jovial comfort to her tone, "The child is not even fully born yet."

Seconds later, Charlotte screamed blue murder as her belly contracted, squeezing Leila's shoulders out. Quicker than the new parents could grasp, Leila popped free, and Duffy caught her up in a soft, and warm towel. Immediately placing the wailing baby to Charlotte's chest the new parents gazed down in awe of their gooey and roaring little creation.

"*14th June 1890*

My Dearest William,

I trust this letter finds you in good health and high spirits, although I know the shadow of Charlotte's absence looms heavily over your heart. I write to you from the shores of England, where the skies have been merciful, and the voyage has been, I dare say, exceedingly pleasant."

William immediately registered the attempted rouse. Eleanore was simpering sickeningly over the pleasantness of the voyage to ease any anxieties he may have and he braced himself for what he knew was coming.

"*Little Leila has proven to be a sea maiden of sorts. She delighted in the gentle sway of the ship and charmed our fellow passengers with her delightful exuberance. I must confess that her laughter was a soothing balm to my heart, which has long yearned for the pitter-patter of a child's footsteps.*"

Trust Eleanore to throw in a jibe over his decision to move from England. He chuckled at the distinct memory of her accusatory words as she screamed in a high-pitched voice about "following some mongrel to Africa!"

"*As for the journey itself, the vessel bore us safely across the vast expanse of the ocean. The days were filled with endless horizons, and the nights, with an endless tapestry of stars. There was a certain serenity in the rhythmic lull of the waves, a reminder that the world endures even in the face of our personal trials.*"

There it is! He flicked the page in smug confirmation to himself - Eleanore simply couldn't resist!

It was with some degree of relief that he reached the end of the page expecting to see well wishes and a sign-off,

"*Now, my dear, I must broach a matter of some sensitivity. It grieves me to bring this to your attention, but you deserve to know the truth. It has come to my attention that Charlotte's family, the Nicholson's...*"

End of the page. His interest peaked, William flipped the page only to find it completely, and infuriatingly blank.

"Well, that's just great!" He mumbled to no one in particular, fully aware that he stood alone in that sunlit room. Although, out of the corners of his eyes, he'd occasionally spot Charlotte standing behind her desk and glaring angrily at him. She demanded that he notice and acknowledge her. But every time his eyes flicked to her, the light glistened and the room stood empty.

"I'm right here, William!" She had yelled at him at every opportunity for the first three days of her appearance, to no avail. Ignoring her, he read through her journals, babbling to himself like a madman in the middle of the night as he drifted through the lonely realm between waking and sleep.

His mind felt terribly disorganised — the unravelling had begun. And he found himself staring down at that letter with no knowledge of how he came to possess it or how long he had stood there deciphering a puzzle with missing pieces.

"*4th June*," He read the date again. It suddenly struck him that Leila had been gone for three whole months. And just as that thought dissolved, he was struck with a new, more intrusive thought: The Nicholson's had been in his home for three months.

Groggily, he shook his head as though to wake himself up but it was no use. The heaviness that lingered constantly behind his eyelids these days swept over him, and he crumpled to the floor loudly as he recalled in flashes stumbling up the staircase to the second landing on the fateful and stormy night of the Nicholson's arrival as Duffy followed frantically behind him.

"You didn't send that letter, did you?" She demanded angrily of him, "They knew nothing of Charlotte's demise!" William turned at the top of the stairs to shoot her a scathing look, soaking and tired. He had spent the day at Blood Rock throwing Charlotte's jewellery off the waterfall and into the pool

Charlotte swam naked in after diving off the edge...

Shaken, Duffy gaped at him and took two steps backwards until her back met the wall of the first landing.

"William!" She breathed at him, concern etched across her beautiful face. But he didn't want to speak about where he had been all day, and he didn't want to fight with Duffy. Though he felt certain he had sent that letter alongside the telegram to his mother.

Standing at the top of the staircase, feet firmly planted on the carpet of the second landing, William asked her, his face cast in shadow,

"Do they know now?"

Taken aback, Duffy nodded her head and took two concerned steps up the staircase towards him. But he turned from her, saying, "Well then." And he turned flippantly toward the passageway but stopped in the centre of the landing. And taking up his usual spot, he laid down flat on his back. William settled himself in for a night of blindly staring at that golden ceiling, willing the floorboards to creek beneath Charlotte's feet, wishing her to pace that study once more.

"They were not upset William." Duffy stood over him, hands on her hips and toe-tapping in annoyance, as he mumbled, "Good - that's good." Distracted, he seemingly slipped off into a catatonic state — for he did not speak for nearly three weeks after the Nicholsons' arrival. Nor did he blink.

In fact, the only times in which William was not catatonic and staring up at that yellowwood ceiling wide-eyed and silent, was when Duffy managed to get him into a bath. With the patience of a saint, she scrubbed his own filth from him, and he repaid her kindness by grabbing at her arms and screaming in her face. In those moments, he appeared terror-stricken and completely lost. Duffy would hold him, dress him and place him back beneath the observatory.

The only thing he ate was dried and stale salt crackers and near rancid peanuts; and he dehydrated himself near to death by drinking until his liver hurt and occasionally throwing his body a bone and guzzling water until he wretched up the poisonous rum.

Presently, William lay weak and seemingly crippled on that observatory floor, unable to account for the gaps in his perception of time. He tasted almonds on his lips and smelled jasmine in the glittering air.

With a panicked mind, he thought about Charlotte, how long would she have been adrift? And Duffy! How long ago had it really been since he last saw her?

His thoughts raced as he cried out desperately to the empty room, "Help me." And he lay there sobbing until his ears picked up the soft creak of the trap door. But William could not see who was crawling up through the portal onto the observatory floor behind him.

And as she slithered closer to him, William's mind registered that the day had grown dark bringing the night. He could not scream, nor could he move as the shuffling sounds of her movements drew closer and closer. Horridly, hands clasped at his arm, feeling their way in opposite directions — left to his shoulder, as the right snaked its way down his leg. With monstrous ease, he felt his knee lift, and his body flip — so that his back rested upon Charlotte's threadbare rug.

With a jolt, he found her face right above his. Illuminated by that god damned golden light. Charlotte was beautiful as ever, and she smiled comfortingly at him as she whispered, "You gave him too much," and she kissed his lips and breathed life into him.

"William?" Her hands touched his face as long locks of her hair fell gently over his face. He flinched and gasped horribly through his dry throat, "Charlotte!" As the gold light turned liquid and sank into his eyes.

Once again, Charlotte kissed him.

Through her lips, he drank hungrily at the water that flowed. Weakly, and with a shaking hand, William reached up and caressed her face. He drank in her honeyed eyes and gaped in astonishment at the golden light flowing so splendidly from her hair.

"William?" She whispered softly to him once again, calling him to her.

She seemed to move like water, and wrap herself around him and suddenly found that he could breathe again. Before his very eyes, she sat up in a seductive straddle. Most peculiarly, she looked straight at the door. Then she dipped down and kissed his lips, and raised herself to remove her night dress. Carnally, she placed her hands in his own, her chest to his chest as that golden light danced melodically from her head. He adored her hips and the way they moved, but he was paralysed and couldn't love Charlotte back.

"Charlotte." His soft whispers begged her to be who she was not, and without hesitation, she slid into that role with villainous ease. Filling up

Charlotte's shape as though it were moulded just for her. With the light being cast out of this circular room, only the moon could betray her and she kissed his lips before he could open his eyes.

"Keep your eyes closed William," Her whispers fell softly on his ears, "do not gaze upon my face."

"But I must!" He begged weakly still. Reaching up, she untied the golden ribbon from her hair and covered his eyes. And he let her. Slowly, he lifted his head, allowing her to gently tie the blindfold until longing overcame him. Finally, the movement found him, and he sat up in haste, pressing his lips hungrily to hers. He was starving, lost without her all this time.

Tenderly, his lips moved from lips to throat as she unbuttoned her blouse. His hands moved gently over her exposed leg beneath her skirts until they rested atop her shapely hips, which began their familiar dance for him. Her responses were beyond her control, his lips sent waves through her, and she rocked for him, filling the lonely void left in the wake of her sister's watery demise.

Slowly, like velvet melting from porcelain, Mary's blouse fell from her shoulders and out of sight as he felt her reach beneath her skirts to unbuckle his belt. Her fingers shook as she unbuttoned his trousers and he whispered sweetly in her ear, "I know you are a dream."

When he awoke in the morning, lying strewn across the observatory floor in front of Charlotte's desk, it was with a ribbon clasped in his hand.

Lifting it to the golden morning light, he examined the familiar light blue hair ribbon more closely. And as he ran his fingers over the intricate stitching of kingfishers and jasmine flowers, a distant memory drifted to the front of his mind. With a sudden vivid pang, he recalled watching Charlotte embroider this very hair ribbon as a gift, right before she set off for England.

Lost in thought and desperate to convince himself, William ran his fingers gently once more over the full length of the ribbon until he found himself smiling coyly to himself. Sheepishly embracing the insane idea that it may not have been a dream after all.

Chapter Eleven

In simpler times, the four friends laid camped out on a picnic blanket beneath the autumn sun. Bellies full to burst on the sumptuous lunches they had all enjoyed with laughter and red wine. And Leila, who propped herself up on her mother's bent knees, gurgling happily as they all chuckled lazily back at her. Feeling fat and well cared for. All around them, bees buzzed, and birds swooped in and out to feast on the various grasshoppers and butterflies as the afternoon sun captured the red fluffy tufts of the grass blooms.

He could have stayed beneath that sun with all of his favourite people forever, completely at peace.

In fact, he visited that place often.

Most days it was the only place he had to go, for over the days and weeks that followed Charlotte's apparition, William's motor functions appeared to fail.

This was first presented with his collapse in the observatory. According to Mary's account, he was found fitting on the floor in front of Charlotte's desk. And as William drank, and sometimes ate everything the Nicholson women provided, his unravelling intensified. Eventually, he rolled down the hill entirely and returned to his catatonic state.

There were moments of lucidity. Brief windows where he appeared to come to, for a few short moments. A moment or a time stamp, but a mark on his brain.

One of these moments presented itself one fateful autumn evening, in the bathtub of all places. Mary, who had taken up Duffy's mantle of bathing him, tiredly ran the sponge over his chest. There was a moment where she froze, staring at his face. At that moment, William appeared to understand where he was. Gazing directly into her eyes, he could not form any words with his slack jaw. But he began to breathe heavily until he could push out a rasping moan.

"William?" Mary whispered gently, "Are you with me?"

And suddenly he could move. Violently, William grabbed her by the arms and screamed in her face, much as he had done to Duffy for the first three weeks of their arrival.

But Mary was not Duffy, "Where is she!" He screamed, over and over again as Mary tried to pull herself free. His wet hands made easy work of her escape. She slipped from his grasp with more ease than expected and fell backwards onto her backside on the slippery bathroom floor where, sobbing and terrified, she crawled from the room. William kept screaming after her as she left, wanting her to never come back. Wanting them all to just leave.

Gasping, he swung his flaccid arm over the edge of their porcelain clawfoot tub and leveraged his weight to pull himself over the tub. Clumsily, he slid wetly over the edge and plopped onto the floor, not unlike a newborn baby.

He took a few moments to catch his breath before he dragged himself from the bathroom, still naked, and out into his and Charlotte's bedroom. Winded, William flipped around and kicked the door shut as he propped himself with his back against the wall.

Muffled through the door, he heard Mary arguing with Catherine loudly on the staircase, only catching the back end of her screeched sentence, "-Broken man! Supposed to provide for myself and this child!"

Catherine's response was harder to hear. She spoke gently to Mary, apparently trying to reason with her, but Mary screamed over her, "Mum! We are not even wed yet and I'm already showing!"

Their footsteps were coming up the passageway now.

"What priest is going to marry us," He could hear her blubbing like a spoiled child, "with him in that state?" Mary finished with a shriek as they came hurrying up the passage toward the bedroom. Catherine made frantic shushing sounds, saying, "Quiet! He'll hear you!"

While Mary stomped ever closer, yelling, "I no longer care!"

With a deafening crash, the door flew open, and she stomped over to William, hooked her bare foot beneath his shoulder and kicked him over so that he lay flat on his back on the floor. Slowly, she knelt down beside him, leaning over him, rather snake-like as her golden hair fell all around his face. And, planting a poisonous kiss on his lips, her fingers tugged loose her embroidered blue hair ribbon and she wrapped the end in her hands. Gracefully, she wound the ribbon around William's throat, and — through gritted teeth, she all but spat in an acid tone, "We'll just have to forge it!"

Before she pulled tight.

Breathless and sweating, William sat up in his own bed, panting and clutching at his bruised throat. Seconds later, there came a thundering up the passage as Mary rushed through the open bedroom door. He felt panicked to see her. Even though her face held an expression of deepest sympathy, illuminated by the candlelight from her hand and reflected on her blond hair. With no trace of hatred or venom in her stare, Mary crossed the small distance between the door and his side of the bed, taking care not to even glance at Charlotte's side. Wishing to avoid another meltdown, she sat lightly on William's side, forcing him to shift over as she placed her candle on the nightstand.

She turned to glance sorrowfully at him, but he was staring at her belly. Trying to discern dreams from reality. There were gaps in his perception of time, and he had somehow been unseated and trapped in a nightmare.

Pretending quite well, Mary placed a cold hand on his cheek, as though checking for a fever. However, instead of drawing her hand back once it became apparent that William had no fever, her hand lingered and she began to caress his cheek instead.

"What are you doing?" He demanded of her, taking her hand roughly and pulling it from his overgrown and unkempt face. In her eyes, he saw hurt among the flecks of gold which hugged the iris. Her eyes looked a lot like Charlotte's, and he almost melted. But there was a cold disconnection in Mary Nicholson's eyes. And he could not unsee the bitter and poisonous glare, or forget the feeling of that ribbon around his throat. She wore it in her hair at that moment. That beautiful gift was handcrafted by his wife right before she left for England...

"She was excited to see you, you know?" William spoke sharply into the dark. Mary, in turn, shifted uncomfortably, not drawing her hand from his very loose grasp. For a short moment, William's eyes left hers and sought a glimpse of her belly.

Perhaps, none of it was real...

But Mary's night frock was far too loose fitting to tell, and she pulled away from him, "I'm not Duffy," she told him angrily again as she stood up and made to leave, "I don't care enough about you to accept this kind of treatment."

Bitter anger bubbled to his throat as she turned to leave his bedroom, leaving her candle behind. He called to her retreating back, “How long has it been since that bad weather was supposed to roll in?”

Pausing at the door, she told him, quite scathingly and reminding him of that cold nothing he had seen behind her eyes, “If you can’t keep track of the time, it’s your own problem, William.”

And as she swept from the darkened room, William caught the faintest glimpse of a slightly rounded belly beneath her loose-fitting night frock.

He waited to hear the guest bedroom door click quietly shut before weakly slipping out of his bed. William left the candle behind, still lit — and he tiptoed down the passageway towards the staircase.

Once he reached the ladder to the observatory, he began his slow climb, which took everything in him to complete. He did not need to unlock the door, for Charlotte stood there to hold it open for him. Smiling at him sweetly, she helped him through the trap door, where, tiredly — he rolled onto the floor. He felt as though his muscles had atrophied.

“They’ve kept you asleep for weeks.” Charlotte whispered to him as he caught his breath on the floor, “I thought you’d go find her after I gave you the letter.” And he suddenly remembered how he got a hold of the letter from his mother...

It had been stolen from the garden gate while he sat in a drunken heap on the observatory floor sobbing pathetically over Charlotte's journals and tearing the pages out...

But when had that happened? And was it real?

“It was real, my love.” She whispered gently to him, caressing his face, and she kissed him gently, “Come back to earth.”

She called these words familiarly to him, just as she had done many times before. At the breakfast table, he selfishly sat daydreaming about ice climbing and tundra. For a long time, his greatest desire consisted of leaving to go far far away. Where he could study the strata that formed the world’s highest peaks more closely.

"Don't you see?" He whispered to her from a blanket beneath the Palestinian sun. With beautiful mountains as their backdrop, she sunned her naked back and giggled at him rather childishly, as he spoke of layers and pressure.

"Look at the straight lines in the rock formation," He told her, "each is a layer of sand that solidified to rock at different points in time."

And yelling, he waved his arms wildly and excitedly at the vast expanse, "Nature's layer cake!"

He was ungrateful at times, missing the mountains and high altitudes the two had given up on upon the birth of their daughter, if only until her small legs could carry her up a mountain.

The laughter echoed through his slipping mind, plummeting William back to Earth - where there was work to be done. Horrified at how easy it was to slip and, rolling onto his side, William glanced up the room at the shelf of Charlotte's black leather-bound journals to find a devastating sight. All but one of the fifteen of her chronicled years since her escape from delirium (and his ascent into it) lay torn to pieces in a concise pile near the deep green lounging chair.

“I'm so sorry,” He choked at her, his tears beginning to flow, “I've ruined your books.” And she smiled more sweetly at him still, taking his hand gently in her own before hauling him to his feet.

“You've not been yourself.” She whispered in a gentle comfort, as they walked together to the repaired window to gaze down at her jasmine. The beautiful blooms now spread across the garden wall. As though he had never ripped the vine from the stone.

“I'm supposed to be the hysterical one, you know.” Charlotte laughed and shot him a mischievous smile to make his heartbreak all over again.

“I miss you terribly.” He croaked through a sore throat as Charlotte examined the bruise with a look of horror on her face, “Look at what they're doing, William.” Tears rolled fatly down her cheeks as she spoke tenderly to him in the darkness.

“Please," He whispered lovingly to her, "don't cry,"

And her pulled her to him in an embrace that he could not feel for he was not real. Yet he relished in it, nonetheless.

When she next spoke again, it was from behind him. And he whipped around to see her standing next to the pile of shredded diaries in the darkest corner of the rounded room.

“Find her, William.” She told him sternly from the shadows, “You're wasting time!”

Without a moment more hesitation, William strode to the trapdoor and lowered himself to the ladder where he silently climbed down and crept down the stairs and out the front door into the front garden as the warm berg winds of the early morning rustled the jasmine and pelted him in the face with the heavenly scent. Time caught him around his bruised throat and shook him awake once again, reminding him to get moving. That he was slipping, once again.

Alarmed, William opened the ill-maintained garden gate and wondered just how much time had slid by him. The rotten state of the gate indicated that he had drifted entirely through the rainy season. Perhaps he had lost his mind entirely... And, since Edward knew nothing about anything, no layers of turpentine had been applied for protection. The wooden gate, no longer strong or structurally sound, sagged sadly as he pulled it open. And as it swung round, its hinges gave off an almighty and crunchy-sounding screech, alarmingly amplified by the silence of the night.

Heart beating in his throat, William wrenched the gate all the way open and let it rest against the jasmine on the stone wall. He walked swiftly to the shed, and carefully slid the heavy hasps from the doors, readying himself to move quickly. He would need to get a saddle on to Silk in a matter of seconds, certain that the heavy doors would make enough noise to wake the Nicholsons from their sleep.

With an all-mighty roar, the rusted iron hinges ground open. Immediately William felt the gut-punching stench of death blast past him along with a swarm of flies.

Retching and gasping for breath, William fell backwards and crawled crablike away from the rotting carcass that was once his beloved horse, Silk. And He noted, with mounting horror and anguish, that meat had been hacked from her.

It was more than William's stomach could bear. He rolled to his right and threw up in the overgrown, and unkempt pumpkin patch. When he could finally breathe again, he got to his feet, bent once more and wretched up the last of his bile, before straightening to leave. But the kitchen window lit up as Mary loomed suddenly into view. Pressing her face up close to the window and candle in hand, it became rather obvious to William that she could not see him. She could see nothing beyond the flame of her candle, which made her blind to the night.

Steadying his breathing and rapidly beating heart, he moved with stealthy haste only once she turned to move toward the back door, no doubt intent upon finding where their captive had gone.

Like a fool, he had eaten and drank everything they had provided to him, and like a fool, he had fallen prey to these professionals, these swindlers.

"They sought to quell the fire of my spirit with ice baths, restraints and the vilest concoctions meant to sedate my thoughts and I lost track of time entirely for weeks on end." Charlotte's morose words played through his mind on repeat as he ran barefoot in the dark through the opened and rotting gate. Once he was through the gate, William ran flat out up the dirt road to the fork in the lane that would lead him to Langa's kraal. And as he ran, the soil coated his feet in a fine glistening dust that caught the light from the moon and the stars.

Suddenly William understood that he was running on the golden light that had so cruelly plagued him since the day that Charlotte's ship was supposed to come in and he turned his back on the pink and peach horizon when the path forked to the East.

"Find her, William!" Charlotte urged him on, running beside him. Though he only caught flashes of her terrified face out of the corners of his eyes every so often. And he argued with himself about what he was seeing and hearing. Her voice could have been a trick of the wind in his ears. Her face — a trick of the light.

But he kept up the pace, nonetheless, heeding her instruction, all the way to Langa's kraal.

Panting, William skidded to a halt outside of Langa's sleeping hut and knocked frantically on the door, praying to see Duffy's beautiful shining face. Hoping, at the very least, for a frown of mild frustration at the early hour...

Instead, he was met with a bitter fury behind Langa's dark eyes such as he had never seen. And the usually sunny man ripped the door of his sleeping hut open, striding right past William as though he were invisible.

Chapter Twelve

Charlotte's laughter had a magical lightness to it.

When isolated, it was a distinctly beautiful, though lonely sound. Comparable to a bird that flew east instead of south, lost and caged to sing her lonely tune to her captors. Charlotte's friendship grew instantly with Duffy. William often joked that the two were more destined for each other than he was for Charlotte. Their connection was immediate, and laughter became the air shared between the two. One more song was added to the call, and the sound became symphonic in nature. William, who came from a stiff culture, thought them to be silly girls. Silly giggling girls who took nothing seriously. Langa, on the other hand, had other opinions.

"Angels," Langa called them.

The two women formed quite the dream team and were often the first into the tombs on new dig sites. He marked their shared laughter as a melody to settle any disturbed spirit. William marked their shared laughter as hyperactivity and pointed out their unwillingness to sit still.

"Who can stay angry or lost," Langa laughed into William's memory by the light of their first fire at their newly built observatory, "listening to these Angels singing?"

"Do you hear angels, Duffy?" Charlotte teased Langa true to her character, lying on her side with her head in William's lap. She sat up rather cat-like and dramatic as ever, cupping her delicate hand to her ear to gales of laughter from Duffy's end as she sipped her gin with her drum clasped between her knees. Wild women, the two shrieked in a squall of laughter, revelling in the freedom they had claimed for themselves. They indulged in non-convention and frolicked in opposition and nonconformity. Duffy sprayed gin at the flames as laughing, Charlotte howled at the starry sky above them. Through the burst of flame, Duffy laid down a low sturdy rhythm, slapping the skin of her drum while Charlotte swayed like water to the beat.

Beautiful and free as a bird, she sipped her rum fruit juice concoction, and laughed, "I don't hear angels," with her honeyed gaze directed at Langa, "I hear wedding bells!"

Perhaps the decades-long schoolyard flirtation shared between Langa and Duffy had bloomed into a marriage somewhere in the fog of lost time. It may be that Duffy had finally taken her fill of travel... Finally ready for the sedentary lifestyle of a goat herders wife...

Somehow, William didn't think so. He recalled, somewhere in the grey, Duffy's call to get back to work. Heart sinking, his feet pounded the ground with all his might. Frantically, he pulled himself up that eastern hill, catching up with the man who usually donned a sunny disposition. William had fallen behind searching the kraal for Duffy but found the place as abandoned as his observatory.

"Langa!" William, called out to the man, wrapped in his mother's golden blanket. He was already directing his goats out to pasture. Barely needing the motivation provided by the thwack of his whipping vine, the noisy creatures of habit all crowded around his gate bleating excitedly. Each ready to start their day of endless feasting upon the dried golden grasses of the autumn hills. Langa acted as he had before, and marched right past William, pretending as though he didn't hear or see him. Though William could sense the rancour coming off of him in waves, as though he exuded an angry heat.

"Langa, for fuck sake!" He called in frustration as the stubborn man marched out into the veld and the golden hills of the Midlands. But anger is a hell of a thing. Langa seemed unable to contain himself as he turned heel and marched right back at William, pointing his knobkerrie at face level as he did so. Once he was within range, he extended his heavily muscled arm and swung the weapon at William, who parried in a swoop, successfully avoiding what would have been a painful, possibly lethal, blow to the skull. In one smooth motion, William grasped the club and pulled his brother to him. He wrapped his free arm around the resistant man, and growling beneath his beard like a lion, he said, "I am your brother!"

"You are no brother!" Langa yelled heavily in his face and pushed him away, letting go of his knobkerrie. And seething, he stomped off after his hastily scattering herd. Frustrated, William, threw the club to the ground and turned to head back to Langa's hut. Intent upon waiting for the man to cool off so that a rational discussion could be had. But Charlotte appeared as furious as he had ever seen her before and screamed in his face, "FIND HER!"

The shock of her sudden appearance threw him backwards in fright, leaving him weak and trembling in the tall grass. Crawling backwards, William threw himself down the hill. Running flat out right at Langa, he grabbed the muscly man around the shoulders, grasping at the blanket which swept easily from his shoulders as he parried the attack. Dust kicked up around them, as William skidded around to face him again, locking them into a fierce battle of strength and grip. With an unfair advantage, William's bare feet gripped the loose soil as he pushed Langa backwards, giving a roar with his efforts. Langa held the frame and slid backwards half a meter before he was able to push back and gain a solid footing in the loose substrate. For a few moments, the two men held the trim, both pushing, neither one willing to budge before William grunted. Pressing his bare feet into the loose soil, he asked Langa with the respect of his native tongue, "Yini ulwanami mfwethu?"

But as he finished his sentence, Langa's hands gripped his shoulders and his hands gripped Langa's. A scream not unlike a roar escaped from the man he called brother. With the strength of an ox, Langa threw William from him. Smoothly scooping and lifting his knobkerrie, he brought it powerfully to the ground where William's head would have been seconds before had he not rolled out of the way.

"Ulethe izitha la?" Langa screamed into the short distance between the two men, pointing toward the observatory. He stepped forward and deflated, "You brought them here!"

Tearfully, Langa dropped the club as he walked closer to William and fell to his knees in his veldt. "You brought them here and he took my woman," the pained man breathed at him hopelessly, and added, "took everything from me."

Cautiously, William approached his friend and knelt before him and drew level with his anguishing face. Langa turned his face to and avoided his eye. But William used his hands to turn the pained face of Langa Mkhize to meet his own.

"Where is she, brother?" He could not speak in more than a whisper. The two men knelt in the misty veldt in the silence of the morning as the sun burst suddenly from behind his observatory on the far neighbouring hill to the west.

Langa's tears rolled fatly as his hands gripped William's arms. But his eyes remained wide and terrified. Comprehension dawned upon them both simultaneously as the gold light of the sun crept down their faces.

Unblinking Langa asked William in the silence of the new morning, "Did my woman not marry that slow man?"

Opposite him, William shook his head.

"No," he said gruffly, "she'd never marry Edward."

He felt stupid and slow, and there were gaps he could not fill. But this was something he was absolutely certain of.

"Day's ago," Langa began to shake as he spoke, "I came to call on Duffy." He swallowed hard and looked William directly in the eye, struggling to breathe past the lump that had choked him for days.

"I saw you standing there," Langa pointed over the hill toward the observatory, "with your eyes empty." The tears swelled in his throat and his voice grew thick, "I called to you!"

Shaken and moved to tears, William stared at his friend, horrified that he couldn't recall such a thing.

"I called you, and you turned from me!" Langa placed his fist powerfully to his chest as the tears and terror overflowed from his eyes.

Burdened, William sighed heavily as Langa took in the sight of him. From his greasy hair and dirty clothing to the purple bruising around his throat.

"I can't explain it, dear friend," William whispered, standing to face his observatory, "but I fear that I've been taken in."

At the tail end of his sentence, and without warning, he began to run down that hill, back toward the observatory. Abandoning his flock, Langa joined him and matched his pace with ease. Both men understood and felt the chill radiating through them as one.

They cut across the hills and ran straight for the observatory, relentlessly keeping pace. Once they reached the observatory, it was time to stay low.

Stealthily, the two men crept out of sight. They skirted the stone wall from the eastern-facing side all the way round to the southern gate.

Catching their breath silently, the two men leaned their backs against the stone wall, cushioned by Charlotte's prized pink jasmine. With bees already working around them and a vine snake or two, the men caught their breath. William breathed deeply the scent, as though filling himself up, before readying himself to move. Slowly and carefully, he raised himself from the wall to his haunches.

Raising himself to sneak a glance over the wall, he scanned first the observatory window above, with the telescope still facing south, and found that it was empty. Obvious danger cleared, his eyes now moved to Leila's bedroom windows, opened to let in the morning breeze — but stood empty, so far as he could tell.

Then he raised himself a little more to scan the ground level, noting that the shed had also been closed back up. None of the Nicholsons lingered in the garden or lurked in the windows. It was time to move.

Standing upright, William motioned to Langa to follow him and he took off running along the grassy side of the dirt road.

As they moved, the sense of urgency began to settle over them more still. William's eyes began to highlight shapes in the dirt path beside them — shapes which resembled bootprints. The boot prints of a large, slow man.

"Be on your guard." William breathed when they took a drink in the tree line near a small creek, "He's lumbering around looking for me."

"Can't you just kill him?" Langa shot back, annoyed and ready to keep going. Cold terror now flowed through his arteries in place of the life-saving blood. William looked up at him, a sadness in his eyes that brought fury to Langa, "I fear I should have."

He sipped hard from his flask and coughed the air into his lungs. They didn't rest long, and he only took one sip to avoid a stitch in his side.

Desperately, the men called out to her, hoping to find her gravely injured, but expecting the worst. They began to search ditches and divots on the roadsides for any clues or signs that Duffy had been there.

They didn't encounter Edward, and his bootprints disappeared off the path around ten kilometres from the dorp.

Madly, the two men ran through the dorp asking anyone and everyone they passed if they had seen Duffy pass through. And with every shake of the head or polite refusal — the two grew increasingly more frantic. Quickly, a horrid certainty cemented within the men that Duffy had not even made it to the first town with her murderous entourage.

Wasting no time, the men returned up the path they had come in from and continued searching devotedly in every place they could think of until they reached the train tracks. With a sinking soul, Langa spotted Duffy's high-heeled leather boot in the gravel alongside the lane switcher. He froze so suddenly that William ran into the back of him, nearly knocking him over when he, too, spotted the weather-worn boot he suddenly remembered seeing Duffy wearing that fateful day.

Horror engulfed the two men as they split off and searched the surrounding area and brush.

It didn't take them long to find her.

Doctor Duffy Duduzile Dlamini had been dressed in that pretty yellow dress when she left to take them back, perhaps intent on heading back to see Langa after all...

They had barely even buried her, the lazy sods.

Discarding her in an already-formed ditch, they had merely piled some rocks on her and left a lot exposed. As a result, bits of her had been eaten away by the wildlife, and what remained was feasted upon by worms and maggots.

As soon as he clapped eyes on the bones of her exposed hand and wrist resting upon the horrible brown stains of what was previously a light and flowy yellow cotton dress, he was rocked with the sudden urge to vomit. Charlotte had picked out that fabric in India. Heartbreakingly he recalled her exclaiming how beautiful it would look against Duffy's skin. And she hand-sewed that stunning dress specially for her chosen sister.

He couldn't let Langa see her this way. Charlotte appeared to share that sentiment, for she peered frantically around out of the corners of his eyes at the sounds of Langa's running feet.

"Stop him!" She cried to William, "Don't let him see!"

But it was too late, Langa ran right through her, a look of utter devastation on his face. His eyes met Williams, and he laid eyes on the horrendous sight behind the man he called brother.

"Don't look," William swallowed hard and stepped up to Langa, grabbing his hands and his face, "Don't look at her brother," he told Langa in gruff tones, "look at me!"

But as the shock wore off, and Langa's brain began to process the horrifically final concept of his lover's death, he became unfrozen. Falling to the dirt beneath his feet, Langa's knees refused to support him any longer as a sound of utter devastation rose from his throat. He screamed out the loss of the woman he would never get to call his wife.

As he screamed, he stood abruptly and picked up one of the heavier rocks from the pitifully disrespectful tomb they had encased Duffy in. Effortlessly, Langa raised that rock high above his head, giving William the dreadful feeling that he was about to be attacked for the heinous crime of bringing this evil into Langa's world. A crime for which he was entirely guilty.

But as Langa launched that rock right at Williams's head, he flinched like the coward he was and dropped. The small boulder sailed right over his head and sank, instead, into Edwards's face with a sickening crunch. Still screaming, Langa picked up the bloodied boulder smoothly as he advanced on the slow man, who had crumpled immediately and now choked on the teeth that had been launched into his throat by the hard blow.

Dripping with acrimonious rage as thick as honey, Langa pinned the rasping slow man to the ground, pressing his knee to Edward's sternum. He stopped screaming as he brought that heavy rock down again and again, ignoring the blood that now dripped from his head and shoulders, until Edward's face caved in wetly, now minced pulp with sharp bits of skull fragments spread out over the grey stones of the train tracks..

Chapter Thirteen

This night, I pen what may be my final entry within these pages, for I stand at the precipice of a decision of such permanence, that it will, with absolute certainty, forever alter the course of my life. I know what my choices are diary. I can choose to play a smiling fool, clapping at the dullest humour and remain blank behind the eyes - I'm getting so good at it, after all. Or, I could choose to continue my silent rebellion and take the hysterectomy.

Somehow, I cannot find favour with either option diary.

For I would very much like to one day mother a daughter as wild and free as I wished to be, but I hold no love for the domesticated life and I grow more panicked as the date nears. It feels unfair to have such a choice thrust upon me before I am even a woman. Nonetheless, I have decided...

I have decided to run, dear Diary.

To take on a life of buccaneering, at least until I earn enough for an apartment in London. I will disguise myself as a man and study at Oxford University, this is a promise which I am committing to your pages, for I choose freedom.

This night, under the cloak of darkness, I shall escape the confines of this suffocating existence where brothers marry sisters who misbehave and drive all potential husbands away. On this night, with a heart-pounding drumbeat of adventure, I take you with me — even if the plan should fail and we plunge into the icy depths together.

Yours in freedom or death

Charlotte

They built her pyre high beneath the open skies so that Duffy could rest beneath the stars, where the golden sparks carried her spirit to the atmosphere. Lovingly and through utter devastation, Langa wrapped her in his golden Basotho blanket, his only remaining treasure and link to his maternal culture.

Overcome by grief, the two men laid their torches on the hay stuffed at the foot of the structure which housed the sleeping frame of Duduzile Dlamini.

Affectionately nicknamed Duffy by the many sailors and dock workers, now retired to the Midlands further inland, leaving the houses closer to the coast for the younger men who could still lift a barrel or a hammer.

Many wandering eyes had frequented her tavern with wives and hungry babes waiting at home for them. Many slapped straight to glance back homeward by the loud-mouthed, no-nonsense Duffy Dlamini - a noted historian and celebrated scientist in a time where neither was allowed. Like her best friend, and chosen sister, Charlotte Nicholson - Duffy Duduzile Dlamini defied, so rebelliously, the constraints of normality and standard.

"Go on and tend to your flock, brother," William told Langa gruffly, shoving him gently away as they neared the gate to the observatory. With golden lights ablaze in every window, except the circular room above, he smirked bitterly at the sentiment that the intruders still had not gained entry back into that sacred place. With a final push, he whispered urgently to Langa, "Go quickly, and never set your eyes on this cursed building again!"

But Langa did not heed the instruction and retreat to his goats, probably scattered all about the hills. Instead, he turned back to the broken man and stared him intently in the eye. Understanding this to be the last time he would lay eyes on William, perhaps until his dying day.

In the haze of Charlotte's prized jasmine, Langa pulled his friend into a monstrous bear hug but found that he had no words to give William.

All was lost.

Burn It

William watched him leave for a long time. The setting sun ahead of Langa cast its dying rays directly into the observatory. The pestilential golden light, a lifelong vexation, drew his gaze as though guiding him by the chin. She appeared in the window, a beautiful shadow beside the brass telescope aimed southwards.

Awestruck, and heart beating in his throat, William watched as Charlotte's silhouette pointed, and he turned carefully to heed her instruction. Faintly, he could hear the panicked bleating of one of Langa's goats which had wandered off a small ledge on some nearby cliffs.

A silly kid, the goat had very clearly seen the cliff as a good climb and now stood trapped, though unharmed a few metres below, bleating feverishly for its mother — currently nowhere to be found.

"Feed them!" Charlotte whispered furiously in his ear, as he peered down at the panicked goat, "Feed them what they have been feeding you."

About an hour later, William trudged home in the dark with the fresh kill slumped loosely across his shoulders. The two women, stood anxiously awaiting Edward's arrival and rushed to the sound of the opening gate. All but bounding through the door to meet him in the garden. William supposed they must have been waiting on the stairs, and he barely suppressed the laugh that escaped him at the look on their faces. Almost falling backwards up the stairs at the shock of seeing him stride through that sagging gate, a mad smile playing across his face.

"William!" Catherine exclaimed in barely suppressed surprise as Mary nodded fervently and rather unconvincingly beside her, "Edwards has been out all day looking for you!"

His unnatural smile widening, William lifted the dead kid loosely from his shoulders and adopted a tone of celebration, "Excellent!" He told the two breathless women, "He'll probably be starving when he gets in."

Adopting Duffy's bossy manner, he ushered the two stricken women inside. With unsuspecting ease, he wove them a tale about seeing the dead horse and going off to find them some food, not mentioning a word of Duffy's corpse or Edward's sloppy, and well-deserved demise.

At the mention of the horse, the two became rather sheepish and shared a look that William pretended not to see as he carried the goat to the kitchen.

He let their panic and fear permeate as he searched his kitchen drawers for the twine, which he then wrapped four or five times around the goat's back legs.

He then used his hunting knife to cut the twine as he turned to face the two women who had previously been engaged in a silent but frantic discussion behind his back and who both snapped their mouths shut. Waiting for him to give up the game. Everyone was playing now.

Smoothly and impassively, he looked both women full in the face, gathering a bucket from next to the wood stove as he swung the young goat up to a hook on the rafters above. And in one fell swoop, he slit its throat. Silently, he wiped the blood from his blade, returning it to its holster behind his jacket as he swept from the room.

Absolutely terrified, the pallid women rushed out of the kitchen behind him, leaving the kid to bleed loud drops into that metal bucket. William paused on the staircase, still smiling that mad and unpleasant smile.

Most horrifyingly, his eyes fell upon Mary.

In an unnaturally pleasant tone, William requested she, "Fetch some of Charlotte's prized jasmine from the wall and make a pretty setting for the table." With a mortified squeak, Mary clicked into motion and rushed past the staircase beneath him and out through the front door. Still smiling, William turned to Catherine, who gulped and shrank beneath his gaze.

"And you too mum." William's tone fell a bit flat, "Why don't you gather some tomatoes and fresh garlic from the garden to put in our stew?"

Wide-eyed, Catherine said nothing, but she too swept past the star case, intent upon getting through that front door and out into the garden where she could speak with her daughter.

But as she reached for the door handle, she felt a sharp tap on her shoulder. Terrified, she suppressed the sudden urge to scream as she turned to find him standing right behind her. He had moved so silently behind her. It was unsettling...

"Perhaps some carrots and potatoes, as well." William nodded at her, that unnatural smile still stapled to his face. Panicked and shaken, Catherine found the door handle behind her. Quick as a flash, she skidded down the front stairs and went haring out into front the garden. Terrified that he would follow her, that he meant to kill them.

Once he was bathed and cleaned off the filth from his eventful day, William unlocked the trapdoor. He vanished into the observatory for a few minutes. Emerging through the ceiling clutching a black leatherbound book. The only one of Charlotte's diaries that he had not torn to shreds and added to that pile next to the lounging chair.

As his left foot made contact with the carpeted floor of the second landing, he stared up intently at that yellowed ceiling. Visibly and with a dull creak, the floorboards began to move. William felt the air move into his lungs, finally having the permission to breathe as Charlotte paced in her study above him, waiting for the dinner party to end.

With clear intention, he moved down the stairs, donned his black apron and smiled at Mary. He gave thanks as he skinned the dead and bled goat, wet hair still slicked back.

"Ah!" William exclaimed explosively into the tense silence that swelled in that kitchen and caused the women to jump in terror. He was gazing across the counter at the various bowls of chopped ingredients including onions, garlic, carrots, potatoes and herbs, "You've chopped up the herbs and veg for me!"

He shifted his attention to Catherine, who stood stiffly next to Mary, seemingly trying to melt into the wall behind her. She made a feeble attempt to counter with her own warm smile, but she was absolutely terrified. It showed on her face and in her eyes.

"Of course, dear William!" She choked up shakily, stepping round the table. And offering a reassuring nod to Mary, who stood frozen in terror behind the table, plainly unsure about what to do with herself, while her mother tried her luck, "Why don't you allow us-,"

But William tutted at her, silencing her at once and waving the large cleaver at her. He placed a bloody finger to his lips.

"Don't be silly," he told Catherine in swollen undertones, "the two of you have cared for me," he butchered the goat as he spoke. Every now and again his words would be interrupted by the unpleasant thud of the meat cleaver on the cutting board, severing bone and sinew with a grunt of effort.

"The least I could do," he told the terrified women after hacking the goats hip and pulling the leg off with a clean but sickening sort of pop, "is return the favour before you leave in the morning."

As he said this, Catherine's eyes shot up from the ground, glassy-eyed. Sensing her curiosity, William smiled at her as he brought the cleaver down hard, severing the hoofed foot of the goat from the sumptuous leg.

"You may have killed my horse," He chuckled madly at her, "but I managed to commission a buggy when I stopped by the town earlier today."

Stunned back to silence, Catherine appeared to swallow any questions or protests she may have had. She stepped back into line beside Mary whose horrified eyes never once left the bunches of jasmine in the vase. A centrepiece which pulled the table setting together rather nicely, in William's opinion.

He made sure to use all of the chopped ingredients and scraped every bit of the herbs into the bubbling stew once the meat had browned beautifully in fried garlic and red wine. The juices released, sent aromas through the air that had stomachs rumbling in desperate discomfort within the hour. The three sat in tense silence for the first fifteen minutes as William plied them each with a glass of red wine. He then picked up that strangely familiar leather-bound book.

Silently, he opened the book and began to read, losing himself until the stew began to smell like it was burning. He appeared to come out of a daze. That eerie, unnatural smile returned to his face as he served them the steaming hot stew, not bothering to dish up a serving for himself.

Madly, he began to laugh into the silence at the horrified expressions on their faces and he told them jovially, "Eat up, ladies!" He laughed, "Eat the food that you have been feeding me for months!" And when they did not move, his temperament shifted from jovial and mad laughter to sharp anger and he yelled as he brought his hand crashing to the yellow wood of the table, "EAT!"

"I'm pregnant William!" Mary sobbed in desperation, hoping to garner sympathy with the devil at this point, "It's yours." She whispered softly through the silence that swelled at that table. But the revelation didn't seem to have the desired effect.

In a low, dangerous growl, William commanded them to eat. His face to shadow and his features became unreadable. The threat was evident. The game was up.

Through their horror-stricken sobs, the two women began to eat the sleeping herbs they had laced him with for months. Through choking cries and snotty coughs, they shovelled the stew down until William called a halt to the sickening display. Smiling widely, he ushered the two upstairs. Bewildered and swaying from the morning glory drops William had laced through the wine. Wine that he had practically poured down their throats. Laughing like a hyena, he guided the unsteady women to their shared bed in the second guest bedroom.

Before he could leave, Catherine caught him by the elbow, demanding to know about Edward's whereabouts through slurred words. He unhooked her arm from his shoulders, and let her fall drunkenly to the crisp white linens Charlotte had brought in from Egypt.

"Where is he?" She demanded of him, her eyes rolling madly in their sockets as Mary fell asleep almost immediately, beside her. William knelt down in front of her, opened his book and read out in front of her face, "This night, under the cloak of darkness, I shall escape the confines of this suffocating existence where brothers marry sisters who misbehave and drive all potential husbands away."

Pointing at the obvious bump beneath Mary's nightgown, he whispered,

"That is not my child."

"When is my son coming back?" Catherine pled pathetically, hardly able to fight the drug-induced sleep that must claim her. And as her eyelids slid heavily shut, he smiled at her and whispered softly in tones of comfort, "He won't be coming back."

Without another word, William left the guest bedroom, quietly shutting and locking the door behind him. Cool as a cucumber — he strode slowly up the passageway, beneath the creaking pacing of Charlotte's feet on the yellowwood floorboards in the observatory above. He stepped out onto the second landing beneath the trap door and delighted himself a few moments in gazing upwards at those pacing strides. Pacing strides that drew further and further apart as she came running across the ceiling above him, just as she had done days or weeks before.

And just as she should have fallen right through the trapdoor into his arms — she dropped to her knees, crawled to the opening and peered down at him.

He could not see her face. That fucking golden light shone blindingly behind her. Melodically, she whispered his name into the silence between the floor and ceiling.

"They are here for the house, William!" Her voice rasped from the opening above him, "You can't let them have it."

"What shall I do?" He asked of her desperately, wishing to climb up and kiss her once more. At these words, Charlotte moved unnaturally through that trap door. Crawling head first down the ladder and straightening herself before him. Away from that blinding golden light that haunted his every waking moment, as well as his dreams.

Beautiful fury etched across every part of Charlotte's face glistened in the dark silence of that house as she stared William in the eye and spoke clearly the words: "Burn it!" Without question, William marched down those stairs and out the front door.

But he did not veer left to open the now sagging wooden gate, instead, he took a deep breath and hauled the barn doors open, exposing, once again, the rotting carcass of his beloved horse, Silk.

He moved with an eerily precise haste. Grabbing a hay bale up in each fist, he lugged them both with ease back into the house, where he spent a bit of time breaking them apart and spreading the hay across the stone floors and up the staircase to the carpeted second landing that didn't need any assistance to burn.

Calmly, William strode to the kitchen, drew the bunch of keys off of the hook near the doorway — which led into the first landing and shuffled through them a short while before finding what appeared to be the right one.

He locked the back door. Picked up his fire tongs and opened the still-smouldering wood stove. All it took was one hot coal, one smouldering ember to ignite the straw surrounding the kitchen.

With organised haste, William made his way through the front door, which he locked behind him too. He expected her to be waiting for him out by the jasmine. When he peered around the moonlit garden, however, he stood a solitary sentinel in the amber glow of the house, currently going up in flames.

William left the place ablaze whispering, "I'll find you, darling." Again and again, until his throat dried out. Reaching the docks twelve hours later.

With the early afternoon sun beating down on him. William sought to wait for Raul over at the Iron Pig.

He quenched his thirst on a pint at the bar next to the mute tradesman, Serge and bought them each another. Serge picked up the flagon and raised it to William, who promptly told him, "Shut the fuck up, Serge!" Before he turned to Tom behind the bar and asked, "When last did you see Raul?" He felt a distinct fluttering in his chest as the spirit of adventure ignited behind his eyes.

But Tom shot him a concerned look instead and, still polishing the same glass he'd been working on since William's first beer, he said, "Have you gone mad?"

Bewildered, William turned a confused look about the empty place. People bustled past on the docks outside, though not a soul darkened Tom's doorstep that day, aside from William and Serge.

Sighing heavily, Tom flipped his dish rag over his shoulder and placed the glass down on the bar. Then he leaned on his tattooed knuckles and sucked air in through his teeth. Shooting William a suspicious squint as though he thought William must be pulling his leg Tom held his stare for a few moments. But when William continued to stare at him through a cloud of confusion, Tom's face fell, having finally decided that William was not having him on. With a heavy heart, he sighed and pushed the words through the gelatinous air between them.

"William," Tom breathed behind yellow teeth, "Raul perished in the shipwreck that took your wife."

The End

Don't miss out!

Visit the website below and you can sign up to receive emails whenever Dihn Bailey publishes a new book. There's no charge and no obligation.

https://books2read.com/r/B-A-MXZZ-PHSOC

BOOKS 2 READ

Connecting independent readers to independent writers.

Did you love *The House That Charlotte Burned*? Then you should read *The Mists of Zealotry: A Tragedy Beneath*[1] by Dihn Bailey!

[2]

In the picturesque town of Ivorton, nestled amidst pristine rivers and veiled by misty mountains, a foreboding presence casts its threatening shadow. The tranquility shattered by a haunting accident —a botched exorcism, leading to the untimely passing of a young girl not yet eighteen. Yet, the villagers remain ensnared in denial, choosing to ignore their role in the tragic events, while an unsettling unease pervades the air.

Whispers and conjectures intertwine like tendrils of fog, weaving tales of a malevolent force unleashed. Rumors persist that the father of the perished girl, driven to madness, took his own life and, in his final act, beckoned forth a dark entity that now lurks over the town. Fear tightens its grip on the townspeople, even as they strive to maintain a façade of normalcy in the face of growing dread.

In this inaugural chapter of the Devoted Ones Trilogy, masterfully weird

---

1. https://books2read.com/u/mgRlwv

2. https://books2read.com/u/mgRlwv

Horror Author Dihn Bailey conjures a mesmerizing tapestry of horror, entwined with romance and shrouded in enigma. Within the cobwebbed corners of Ivorton's secrets, a darkness not yet primed for revelation dwells. In the Mists of Ivorton, the true darkness of the human condition will be revealed.

Prepare to embark on a journey where the boundaries between the living and the ethereal seemingly blur, and the fragile equilibrium between life and death hangs in the balance. This first installment, a masterstroke of chilling suspense, offers no closure, leaving your senses yearning for more, and your mind haunted by lingering questions. Will you dare to step into the mist and confront the truth that awaits, or will you remain bound by the allure of the unknown?

About the Author

Dive into chilling worlds crafted by the mouthy south African and indie horror author Dihn Bailey. With an electrifying debut in 2023, Dihn Bailey has already left an indelible mark on the literary landscape. In 2023, Dihn ventured fearlessly into the realm of indie publishing, bringing forth a spine-tingling horror novel that seized the imaginations and stomachs of readers. Her debut work, "The Mists of Zealotry: A Tragedy Beneath" and latest release, "The House That Charlotte Burned" are both testaments to Dihn's unique ability to transform the ordinary into the macabre, and spin as much discomfort out of it as possible! She weaves tales that haunt the mind and offer no closure long after the final page. But this is just the beginning. With several more bloodcurdling projects currently in progress, Dihn Bailey is poised at the very beginning of a lifelong dedication to the literary arts. Each word she puts to paper, a deliberate step into the unknown, inviting readers to confront what really makes them squirm and embrace the thrill of the eerie and unexplained.

Milton Keynes UK
Ingram Content Group UK Ltd.
UKHW011115201123
432909UK00001B/47

9 798223 24879